ON THE CREST
OF A WAVE

Other books by Fran McNabb:

Once in a Half Moon
A Light in the Dark

ON THE CREST
OF A WAVE

•

Fran McNabb

AVALON BOOKS
NEW YORK

Published by Thomas Bouregy & Co., Inc.
160 Madison Avenue, New York, NY 10016

Library of Congress Cataloging-in-Publication Data

McNabb, Fran.
    On the crest of a wave / Fran McNabb.
        p. cm.
    ISBN 978-0-8034-9996-6
    1. Southern States—History—Civil War, 1861–1865—
Fiction. I. Title.
    PS3613.C5856O5 2008
    813'.6—dc22
                                                    2009024261

PRINTED IN THE UNITED STATES OF AMERICA
ON ACID-FREE PAPER
BY HADDON CRAFTSMEN, BLOOMSBURG, PENNSYLVANIA

For the McNabb boys—Donald,
Thomas, and Connor

Chapter One

New Orleans
April 1864

N o one noticed the mosquito that lit on Vivian Marie's white neck. No one cared if Matilda's robe barely covered her ankle or Lucille's hair comb dangled from her long golden mane.

No one paid attention to the girls who hung over the balcony of the Riverside Theater and joined in the roar from the melee below. Two young soldiers circling each other in an age-old choreography of defending their masculine honor drew the attention of everyone standing in and above a New Orleans alley just blocks away from the Mississippi River.

Moments before the men were part of the audience, but now they strutted and bobbed within the crowd of loud spectators waiting for the right moment to strike.

Men in the outer circle yelled for the action to begin, then cheered as one soldier jabbed the other in the nose. He fell back into the crowd. An onlooker grabbed the stunned man by the shoulders, spun him around, then shoved him back into the other soldier's fist.

The crowd loved it.

The women above squealed.

The two soldiers were the diversion tonight, entertainment away from the reminders of war.

Major Jake Warren, standing away from the crowd, pulled a cigar from his uniform, lit it, then turned his back on the chaos.

These weren't his men, and this wasn't his city any longer.

Yellowed street lamps, shrouded in a thick southern fog, barely lit the sidewalks along Canal Street. Picking his steps carefully, Major Warren turned the corner and walked away from the brawl that threatened to involve him in a night of paperwork and questions if he hung around any longer.

His weeklong visit into the city of New Orleans had come to an end. Now that he'd gotten the needed supplies for his troops, he was ready to get back to his men and his prisoners on the barren stretch of an island in the Gulf of Mexico.

He left the riverfront emotionally drained. After spending the last three months in the sweltering heat on Ship Island overseeing a prisoner-of-war camp, he couldn't believe he looked forward to returning.

Tomorrow morning he'd ride out to an outlying bayou community to make arrangements for a load of cattle and grain, then he'd be free to leave the filth and congestion of the city.

Stepping over a puddle of water from the latest afternoon shower, he headed to the boardinghouse to take advantage of one last night in a bed with clean sheets and no sand. Even the cockroaches in the city didn't match the size or the numbers of those that he fought nightly on the island.

He had learned to give thanks for little favors. Even for a city boy, he looked forward to the following morning when he could smell the rich soil in the open fields.

Camille Rene Hollander propped her trouser-covered leg against the front board of her wagon and strained to keep the old mare on the road.

Rich black dirt, carried from fertile lands to the north and spread by floodwaters of the Mississippi River, was now nothing more than mud from a recent summer squall. On sprawling Southern plantations, the dirt produced valuable cotton and sugarcane, but today the muck sucked wagon wheels into its deep, black soup.

"Come on, girl. You can do it, Nancy. We've been through worse than this." Camille's small hands, covered in well-worn, oversized gloves, communicated with the animal with the slightest flick of the reins. Her voice, soft and soothing, disguised the fear that threatened to cut off her air supply.

With white knuckles, her sister Katherine clutched the wooden bench, letting go only to swat pesky mosquitoes that buzzed around their heads.

"I don't like this." Katherine didn't disguise the fear in her voice. "Where is everyone?"

"I don't know. Just sit still. Maybe we're not as close to the city as I thought." Camille's voice, sharper than she expected, produced the familiar sting of guilt that needled her each time she answered her sister roughly.

Katherine's wide eyes announced an impending flood of tears.

"I'm sorry, Katherine. I didn't mean to yell, but I'm a little jumpy too. I'm not even sure where we are."

Camille turned her attention back to the old mare. "Come on, girl, keep going. That'a girl. You're doing just fine."

Katherine bit a fingernail and spoke quietly. "Mama said over and over not to talk to anyone on this road, to pretend that people didn't exist when we passed them. Well, there aren't any people, Camille. We haven't passed anyone all day. Something's wrong."

"Maybe, but it's too late to turn back now." In her heart, Camille agreed with her sister. She'd been down this road to New Orleans too many times not to feel the difference.

"We have to get to Mr. Taloux's before dark or there

really will be something wrong. I'm not going to be caught out here after the sun goes down. Just relax."

"That's easy for you to say, but I'm scared. These awful clothes are soaked. I smell like a wet dog, and I'm hungry."

Irritation nipped at Camille's nerves. She was cold, scared, and hungry too, but just looking at Katherine made her hide her own fears. Far too young and innocent, her youngest sister shouldn't have to face the hardships the war had caused her family. No words materialized to console her, and no means existed to keep her sister's innocence sheltered.

Managing to get through each day was all Camille knew how to do. At almost twenty-three she'd thought life would be different, but the war had put an end to those dreams. With her brother fighting with the Biloxi Rifles and her father dead, the weight of helping her mother fell on her shoulders. Right now, managing to get the old wagon through the mud to New Orleans pushed aside thoughts of anything else.

Camille patted the rough broadcloth of her brother's trousers on Katherine's leg. Her delicate body should have been clothed in pink silk and lace, not oversized trousers held up with string.

Camille ignored the curses that threatened to escape her and searched for some encouraging words for her sister. "We should be there soon. Maybe Mrs. Taloux will have us a nice bowl of soup and a big glass of milk like she usually does."

Katherine smiled halfheartedly. "I hope she has cake. We haven't tasted cake made with real sugar in a long time."

Camille's mouth watered.

"And Louis. Remember Louis, Millie? He was sooo handsome. Do you think he's still in the house next door to them?"

"I don't know. He's old enough to have enlisted."

Katherine frowned. "I hope not. He said I was pretty. I wonder if Mrs. Taloux will let me wear that dress again. It was so beautiful."

Katherine's eyes glazed over. Camille didn't interfere with her reverie. Pleasure in any form was a rarity. Happy for her sister, she forced a smile and concentrated on keeping Nancy moving.

Gnarled trunks of cypress trees grew thick along the roadside and reached deep into the near blackness of the swamp. Twisted limbs hung close to the road, too close as far as Camille was concerned. How could she not worry? She had spent too many days in the bayous watching her brother shoot moccasins from tree limbs just like these. She swallowed hard and looked away from the dark trees.

"Gettie up there, girl." She flicked the reins, then immediately jerked them back. "Whoa."

"What's wrong? Why are we stopping?"

"Shhh. Listen."

With Katherine clinging to her sleeve, Camille strained to hear sounds from the road ahead of them.

They sat in the still silence, which broke only by the shuffling of the mare's hoofs and the buzzing of the mosquitoes.

Camille pushed several strands of hair under the brim of her large, masculine hat, then reached over and did the same for Katherine.

A low, muffled din floated around the next curve in the road, growing louder with each second. Camille raised the hat brim slightly and stared into the last streams of sunlight on the dirt road. Her heart pounded. Noise like that could only come from a group of men, marching men. Soldiers.

"What do we do?" Katherine's voice, a whispered screech, teetered on the verge of hysteria.

Camille touched her sister's thigh. "Nothing. Just sit still. Don't say a word."

Camille swallowed the bile bubbling in her throat. She gulped each of her breaths. "We're just two boys on a wagon, that's all."

Just as the words passed her lips, a wall of blue coats emerged ahead of them. Instantly throwing themselves into action, the soldiers filled the narrow road. Some fumbled with rifles before aiming at the wagon. Some fell to their knees and took aim, creating an armed barrier across the narrow road.

It all happened in a matter of seconds, but to Camille, the action happened in slow, exaggerated motions. Each soldier raised his weapon and aimed directly at them. This time Camille tasted the bitter bile.

The old mare stopped and for a long, agonizing moment, no one moved. An ominous silence fell over the road. Soldiers stared at the wagon and the two young riders stared at the guns. Finally, a horse and rider broke through the blue coats, stopping a short distance from the mare.

The man, short and squatty, wore a wrinkled blue uniform and crumpled hat, but his pudgy face and twinkling eyes didn't keep the authority from ringing in his voice. "Identify yourself while you still can." His horse, as squatty and square as its rider, stomped his front hoofs and snorted as if to reinforce the order.

Camille tried to speak like the young lads that played on the oyster-shell lanes near her house. "We're from Biloxi, a fishing village in Mississippi. We're on our way to New Orleans to sell stuff for Mama. We only have ladies' clothes and salt in the wagon."

To hide her trembling hands, Camille kept them tucked close to her stomach and hoped the shaking of the reins didn't give her fears away. Her brother's words managed to seep through her muddled brain. "Never let your enemy know you're afraid, Camille. They'll respect you for it." Hoping he was right, she looked straight into the soldier's eyes.

Running a hand across his double chin, the soldier studied her for a moment before jerking his head to signal to the men behind him. At his silent command, three soldiers scrambled to the rear of the wagon.

Camille and Katherine never moved, even when

the wagon creaked and rocked from the weight of the first man jumping into the back. Camille stiffened as she listened to the men roll the slat-boarded salt barrel to the edge of the wagon.

When Nancy pulled at her harness, Camille settled her with a touch to the rein, but she couldn't settle the anger at having Yanks going through the merchandise that represented weeks of intense labor.

Behind her back, she heard the men pry open the top of the wooden salt barrel. Each creak threatened to undo the bravado she feigned. She bit her lip to keep from screaming.

"It's salt all right," yelled one of the men. "Prettiest stuff I've seen in a long time."

Camille yanked her body around in time to see two men jump up on the wagon, making the barrel teeter on its rim. With a slow roll and a flurry of grabbing from the soldier, the barrel crashed to the ground. She squeezed her eyes and hoped the tears wouldn't roll down her cheeks. Weeks of hard work lay in the mud below the wagon.

"Carter!" roared the man on horseback, his eyes no longer twinkling. "We need salt, but not if it's full of mud. If it's just salt in the barrels, we'll take the wagon. Check those packages up front before you ruin anything else."

Camille glared at the men in her wagon, then swung around to face the man in charge. "Please don't take the packages. They're just women's and babies' clothes. Mama sewed all of those clothes herself. We really need them for trading."

"Well, how sweet. The little boys are going to market to trade for their sweet mama." Sarcasm dripped from his lips. "Rip them open. Make sure these Confederates aren't sneaking something into the city that they're not supposed to have." He spit a wad of tobacco.

The men didn't waste any time. Each grabbed a package and yanked away the neatly tucked paper that held together stacks of folded garments.

"Look here, men," the man closest to Camille shouted from behind her. "Sweet little hand-stitched gowns. Now I wonder how this poor Mississippi family got the stuff to make these. Here, Private, your new wife would love to sleep in this even though it was made with Confederate hands." He tossed the gown across the road to a young blond soldier who smiled in gratitude. "Catch, Sarg, your wife could use this dress." He tossed another one, but it fell in a puddle before anyone could catch it.

Rage shot through Camille. She bolted off her seat to face the men in the back of the wagon. "Don't touch another piece." With legs spread apart and hands on her hips, she worked to camouflage her quivering insides with a strong, steady voice.

The two soldiers laughed.

Remembering her sister, Camille squelched the urge to spit on the men and tried reasoning. "I told you my mama sewed those pieces by hand, and we're going to trade them for medicine. Don't ruin them." She dug deep. "Please."

The two men looked at each other, made long faces, then burst out laughing again.

Camille fumed. "They're not yours, so get your dirty, grimy hands off them."

The crowd of men on the ground snickered and hooted. One of the men in the wagon spit on a gown then tossed it on the ground with slow exaggerated motions. As he turned to grab another piece, Camille lunged over the front seat, knocking him off balance. She grabbed the garment from his hand as he sprawled against the side of the wagon.

The rest of the men roared. "Way to go, Carter. We won't tell anyone that you were overpowered by a scrawny Confederate kid."

Wiping the saliva from the side of his mouth, the man they called Carter glared at Camille with hate in his eyes. "You're going to be sorry you did that, boy." He gripped the side of the wagon to pull himself from his twisted position, throwing himself in her direction.

Camille managed to take a couple of unsure steps backward as the soldier grabbed for her. Dodging his wild flailing arms, she lost her balance, slammed against the rough boards of the wagon, and toppled over the side. With a thud, she hit the muddy ground. Air whooshed from her lungs.

"Stop, you'll hurt my sister." Katherine's screams were muffled in Camille's ears, but she knew when her sister stumbled down from the wagon seat and knelt over her.

The soldiers moved closer to the crumpled heap on the ground. Camille's hat lay in the mud and her long ebony hair now covered her face. No one spoke. Katherine pulled her sister up into a sitting position.

Camille brushed the wet hair from her face, spit mud, and gasped for air. Her oversized shirt and pants, now wet from the mud, clung to her body.

"Millie, are you okay?" Katherine's strained voice and enormous eyes shouted fear. She threw her arms around Camille and held tight.

"I think so." But Camille groaned as a sharp pain shot down her arm.

Blue uniforms crowded around the two girls on the ground, smothering them with their closeness. The squatty leader clambered down from his horse and pushed through the circle. "Let me through. Step aside." When he stretched a hand out to Camille, she yanked away from him.

"Keep your hands off me. You've ruined enough already today."

Using Katherine for support, she stood. Camille looked away from the sergeant to the clothes scattered around the wagon, at the broken barrel of salt lying in the road, then at her wet clothes that no longer hid the fact she was a female.

The sergeant crossed his arms over his barrel chest. "Being in disguise, young lady, is grounds enough to be charged with being a spy." The harshness in his voice had softened.

His change of tone did nothing to quell the rage that bubbled within Camille. "A spy? What would I have been spying on? You Yankees don't do anything in New Orleans but frequent the gaming houses."

The answer may have hit too close to home for the soldier. His face burned red. "Sergeant Lindsey, take her and this other one, who I guess is also a girl, and let them ride with you and Private Lewis. We'll take them into town."

"Don't touch us." Camille's back stiffened. She put a protective arm around her sister. "I'll drive us into town. We don't need to be carried in." She pushed her sister toward the wagon.

The sergeant turned to the young soldier and growled, "I said to put them on the horses."

The harshness of his voice threatened to shatter the little composure that Camille clung to, but it wasn't enough to make her be plopped down on a Yankee horse to rub against a blue belly.

"Get in the wagon, Katherine." As she shoved her sister gently and turned to go around to the other side, one of the men grabbed her from behind and spun her around. With an iron grasp, his arm encircled her body beneath her ribs, smashed her body against his, and forced the air from her lungs.

Like a caged animal, she fought against her captive before she lost that last breath of air. She gasped. With the heel of her shoe, she kicked her assailant in the shins, then threw her head back into his chin.

"Woohoo. I've got me a wildcat!" he yelled, but his grip held. "Quit your squirming or you're gonna get hurt."

She heard her sister struggling behind her and felt rather than saw the rest of the men moving in closer. She squirmed. She kicked, but the man squeezed tighter. Through his curses, she heard the other soldiers snicker. Fear for herself and for Katherine threatened to strangle her. She fought for her next breath.

The blast of a rifle silenced the raucous jeers. No one moved. The soldier's arm still clamped her body next to his, but she took advantage of the momentary lull to breathe deeply.

The wall of soldiers stepped back to allow a large black horse through the crowd. A Union officer carrying a rifle in the crook of his arm sat tall and relaxed in the saddle, but a scowl across his face showed his displeasure at the scene in front of him. His gaze moved from the wagon to Katherine before resting on Camille. He stared at her for a long moment then turned to the sergeant.

"What's going on here?"

As the sergeant started his explanation, Camille watched the man on horseback scrutinize her sister. His face showed no expression. When his gaze settled on her, Camille wanted to turn away from his deep blue eyes, but she refused to let a Yankee officer see that she was at a disadvantage. Forcing her head high, she returned his stare and hoped he couldn't detect her distress.

The sergeant finished his explanation. He waited. "Major?"

The major turned his attention to the sergeant. "Thank you. I'll need two men to escort these ladies into town, and I see no reason why they can't ride in the wagon." He looked directly at Camille. "I'm Major Jake Warren. What are your names?"

Enemy or not, the major had just given them a small reprieve. She sat up and tried to answer calmly. "I'm Camille Rene Hollander, and this is my sister Katherine."

"Well, Miss Hollander, just where were you and your sister planning to spend the night?"

Camille ignored the hint of sarcasm in his question and swallowed the string of curses that tickled her throat. He was an officer. He could help them.

"We usually stay at Mr. Taloux's boardinghouse just off Canal Street. There's a mercantile dealer who buys our clothes. He meets us there. We then send our salt to the docks at the riverfront."

The major shifted in his seat. "These are not the safest of times for two girls to be traveling alone."

"I beg your pardon," she cut in. "We've never had any trouble, that is, until today."

Major Warren continued, "I guess no one told you that there's a war going on. Our troops have been in New Orleans long enough for you locals to accept their presence."

Camille interrupted him. "As I said, we've never encountered any trouble before. Your soldiers have always let us into the city and out again." Camille spit out her words, then turned and placed her hand on the wagon, the pain in her arm momentarily making her light-headed.

"Are you injured?" The major didn't wait for an answer. "Sergeant, did your men harm these girls?"

"No, sir. She fell out of the wagon, when, uh, she and one of my men went at it."

"Went at it?" he questioned. "I want the name of your commanding officer, Sergeant." He turned his attention back to Camille. "Is that true?"

"Yes, he was ruining the clothing." She turned and glared at the sergeant. "I had to do something since your sergeant didn't."

Camille couldn't tell if it was the size of the horse or if the man who sat on it was actually as big and menacing as he appeared. She craned her neck to see him clearly, but looking up made her head spin again. She gripped the wagon for support.

"Are you sure you're okay, Miss Hollander?"

Camille nodded. No one moved or tried to help her. For that she was relieved.

After a moment, she looked into the eyes of the major. They were the brightest blue eyes she had ever seen on a man. Even with his cocked hat shading his face, they shone at her. His face was clean shaven, his voice had been raspy, but his eyes showed amusement.

That did it. Her weakness vanished. She couldn't believe that he thought their situation amusing. She opened her mouth to tell him how she felt, but he cut her off.

"Seems you're okay." There was a hint of a grin on his face. "You'll be escorted with your wagon to the boardinghouse. You can keep your clothing merchandise, but the salt will be given to our troops."

Fighting to control the rage that threatened to explode, Camille straightened her frame and found her voice.

"My sisters and I worked for weeks drying that salt. We planned to trade it for medicine. Your troops have always been fair with us, and I'm sure you'll do the same." Camille waited for a response but the officer said nothing, confirming her guess that he was without heart or manners.

"I'm sorry, but I have no choice. We have orders to confiscate what our troops need, and we need your salt."

Even though the major's voice hinted at understanding, she refused to give in. Holding her temper, she tried reasoning. "There're only about four hundred folks left in our village, nothing but old people, women, and children, and a few returning wounded. They're counting on us. We don't have a doctor or any incoming medicine. My mother and I tend to them the best way we know how, but we need that medicine."

A long silence ensued before he answered. "I appreciate your war effort, but I'd be court-martialed for treason if I didn't take this salt for my own troops."

"Take it, but pay for it like a gentleman."

The amusement vanished from his eyes, replaced by an instantaneous flash of sorrow. Did the man understand what she and her sister had gone through? He might be sympathetic, but Camille would not admit to a kindness from a Yankee.

"I took you for a gentleman," she continued, "but obviously you're as bad as these other soldiers." Keeping her left arm close to her body, she bent down to pick up the scattered clothing. "But on behalf of my family, we thank you for the clothes." Her temper flared. She shook each piece of clothing violently, scattering mud on those around her.

The men closest to her took a step away as she stooped, shook, stooped, and shook each piece again. The flying mud landed on her as much as on the soldiers, but her temper didn't allow her to quit.

"I am a gentleman, ma'am." The officer finally said with a half grin on his face. "I could leave you out here and just take your wagon, but, of course, I wouldn't do that to two ladies."

From the corner of her eye, she saw Katherine's hand cover her mouth. A muffled sob followed.

Clinging to the pile of muddy garments in her arms,

she turned back to the major and swallowed the rage in her throat. His words held too much truth to be comfortable.

She hated him for what he stood for. She hated him for making her feel inadequate, but she knew when to stop.

Nonchalantly adjusting the harness on his horse as if what he had said meant nothing to him, he then looked back at her. "When we get to town, these two men will see that your wagon is returned to you after removing the salt."

Camille's mouth dropped, but before she was able to answer, the major turned his attention back to the sergeant.

"Use one of our horses to haul the wagon to the docks. This one looks as if it's about to die from exhaustion."

Camille looked at Nancy and said a prayer of thanks that her poor mare would be saved from any extra hardships.

Camille felt the major's gaze burning into her. She snapped her head back to him.

"The men will escort you out of the city tomorrow morning," he continued. "My advice to you is to lock your door at the boardinghouse, be ready when the soldiers get there, and don't make any side stops as you leave the city."

He spun the horse around, spoke to the sergeant, then galloped off.

Camille stood by the wagon holding her soiled garments in her aching arm. Fuming, she brushed a clump of muddy hair from her face.

Helplessness was not a feeling she dealt with well. She needed to do something, but it was obvious there was nothing that she could do against the Yankee army.

Nothing for now, anyway.

Chapter Two

A sea of blue uniforms flooded the sidewalks and storefronts on Canal Street. Older, experienced soldiers with faded jackets, some torn, some patched, watched silently as Camille's wagon followed the procession of soldiers in front of her.

Camille saw no outward hostility from the soldiers, but their mournful looks from watching their friends die on battlefields reached out and touched her soul. She had seen that same look in the faces of the young men returning to her village.

Younger, clean-cut men with bright blue jackets and stiffly creased hats stood tall and proud, stepping forward away from the sidewalk to tip their hats or to nod ever so slightly as the girls passed by. Slick young faces showing no signs of battle openly flirted.

Katherine raised her hand coyly and waved to a smooth-skinned young man who stepped closest to the wagon as it passed his corner. Camille guessed he couldn't be much older than Katherine's fifteen years. Nevertheless, he was the enemy.

Camille placed a hand on Katherine's leg. "Stop that. These are Union soldiers, just like the ones who ruined our clothes and stole our salt."

"No, they're not, Millie. I'll bet most of them just got here and haven't even seen a battle yet."

"Doesn't matter. They'll be shooting at our men soon enough."

Camille's eyes burned from unexpected tears that threatened to embarrass her. Too young to understand, her sister couldn't see the tragedy here. Camille's chest tightened. These lads would be the perfect age to take her sister to a ball if the times were right, not old enough to shoot their neighbors dead or burn their cities to the ground.

Camille wanted to enjoy the attention of the men, but she sat rigid. She felt nothing but anger from what the war had done to their lives and humiliation at being paraded down the street with mud stuck to her body and hair.

The squatty sergeant pulled his horse up alongside the wagon. "Is that your boardinghouse?"

His voice pulled Camille out of her self-pity. She nodded.

"When we stop, you get your bags and hightail it

into the building and stay there until one of my men comes for you in the morning. There will be a guard at the door so don't try anything foolish."

Camille stared at him.

He continued, "If you're caught on the street, I can't guarantee your safety. You try to escape, and my men won't hesitate to shoot."

"I have no intentions of leaving since you've seen to it that we have nothing to trade. If you remember, sir, you now have our salt, and most of our clothing is ruined."

The man smiled and tipped his hat. "And we thank you for the salt." At that he turned his horse and rode off.

"Blasted arrogance," Camille said under her breath.

It was Katherine's turn to comfort her sister. With a hand on Camille's leg, she smiled. "It could've been worse. They've really been nice."

Camille rolled her eyes and shook her head.

"Nice? They took our salt. All that hard work for nothing. All those hours, days wasted," she fumed.

"But they could've hurt us, Camille, had that nice officer not stopped them."

Camille opened her mouth to argue that the officer was not "nice" as her sister put it, but kept the words to herself.

The procession stopped in front of the Taloux's Boarding House.

"Get the bag, would you, Katherine? Let Mrs. Taloux know we're here. I'll see to Nancy."

A soldier jumped off his horse and helped Katherine to the ground. "Thank you," Camille heard her say as she took the small bag and sashayed up the front steps.

Camille jumped off the wagon unassisted, then untied Nancy's tether. "Come on, Nancy."

Nancy plodded along next to Camille around to the back of the building. Taking one last look at the wagon with her salt, she sighed deeply then led Nancy into the familiar, small stable area and began to remove her reins. The smell of clean, fresh hay soothed her.

Mr. Taloux was having no trouble getting the supplies he needed for his boardinghouse, Camille thought to herself. Union connections probably, but she didn't blame him one bit. Everyone found a way to survive. Selling salt to anyone who would pay the price was her family's way.

"I saw you come in."

Startled, Camille dropped the lead rein and turned abruptly.

The tall major stood inside the doorway, holding his horse by its reins. "Sorry, I didn't mean to startle you. I saw you go around the building alone and wondered why someone wasn't escorting you or taking care of your animal."

Camille found her voice, but it trembled as she spoke. "No one offered. Anyway I'm quite capable of caring for her myself."

"I'm sure you are. I wasn't insinuating that you

weren't. It's not safe for you to be out here alone, and the sergeant will hear about it."

The idea of the obnoxious sergeant getting a tongue-lashing pleased Camille. She turned back to Nancy without commenting.

The major stepped closer to Nancy's stall. "How often do you come into the city?"

Feeling ill at ease, she stepped closer to Nancy and fumbled with her strap. "Not often," she managed to say.

The man was much too close for comfort. It hadn't been only the size of the horse that made him menacing on the road today. Standing near the stall, he now towered over her.

For a moment, she forgot he was the enemy. His dark hair, tanned skin, and clean uniform reminded her of the young soldiers who proudly marched away from the coast with her brother. Many had been prospective beaus. Most would not return. This man too was someone's family, maybe even husband.

She blinked and finished answering his question. "It takes several months for us to collect enough salt to make it worth our while to venture over here."

She stopped abruptly, remembering that no matter how nice-looking this man was or what family he'd left behind, he was fighting for the Union.

She glared at him.

For a long moment he said nothing. The strained silence made her uncomfortable, but she refused to yield. He had followed her in here uninvited. He could leave uninvited.

"Look, Miss Hollander. That was your name, right?"

Camille nodded.

"I'm going to send one of my men in here to escort you back to the house. Don't come out alone again." He turned to go, then stopped. "How's your arm?"

Camille unconsciously placed her hand on her left shoulder. "It'll be fine."

"We have a doctor with us in the house next door. I'll be glad to have him come over to take a look at it."

"Thank you, but I'll be fine. My mother and I help nurse our neighbors. She'll take care of me when I get home."

"If you change your mind about the doctor, send one of the men on guard. Tell them to ask for me, Major Warren, and I'll send a doctor to you." After another silent moment, he tipped his hat and started to leave.

"Major Warren?"

He turned and waited.

She pulled from deep within. It wasn't easy asking a Yankee for a favor. "Would you help us get permission to have our clothing merchant visit today? Even though most of the clothes are muddy, he might be able to purchase a few."

Major Warren squinted, obviously trying to make a decision that would probably get him into hot water with someone.

"We wouldn't leave our room, and if he bought

some of them, the money would be greatly appreciated. Our trip wouldn't be a total failure."

Her heart pounded. If he refused her request, more than the salt and the clothes would be ruined. She swallowed her pride. Stepping away from the horse, she held her hands together in the front of her body as demurely as possible. Muddy, baggy trousers didn't help the feminine look she was trying to achieve, but it couldn't hurt to try.

"Who is this merchant? He may not be in the city any longer."

Camille's palms began to sweat. "His name is Joseph Dedeaux. He has a small shop on Decatur Street, but he'll visit us at the hotel if we get a message to him."

"I'll send someone to see if he's still open for business, and I'll tell the guard to let him through. The guard will remain in the room with you throughout the transaction." He tipped his hat again. "Have a nice stay."

"Sir. If he does buy, we would like to stop at the hospital to purchase medicines. We're in desperate need of quinine and chloroform."

He shook his head. "That I can't do. It's called a war, Miss Hollander, and if I took needed supplies from my own wounded to help yours, I'd be abetting the enemy. You can sell your goods, but you can't stop at the hospital." This time he turned without a good-bye.

Camille gritted her teeth and suppressed a scream of frustration. "Yankee scum," she said under her breath. "Scum, scum, scum." For a moment she stood grimacing at the door of the barn.

Giving in to her emotions, she placed her head against Nancy's warm neck. Tears burned her eyelids. She didn't have the strength to stop them. They flowed freely down her cheeks and onto Nancy's coarse hair. It felt good.

Finally, a cough from the door made her look up.

"Ma'am, I was told to escort you back to the boardinghouse."

A young soldier stood silhouetted against the door frame.

"Thank you." Camille wiped her eyes on her shirtsleeve away from the view of the young man. "I'll be finished here in just a minute."

"Yes, ma'am."

Camille made sure Nancy was well watered and fed. It was the most feed that the mare had had in months.

Smiling, she patted her on the rump. *At least one of us is happy tonight.*

Camille sat stiffly in an upholstered loveseat with Katherine's head nestled in her arms. She listened to her sister talk about their encounter on the road in the hopes that it would ease her anxiety.

With no one to comfort her or help with her responsibilities, Camille held her fears and worries inside. Sometimes life seemed hopeless with no end in sight. How she longed for a young man's arms to hold her close and help her forget the problems she faced each day.

She pulled Katherine close to her. Hope still remained for her younger sisters, but by the time this war was over, Camille knew she'd be too old to be wanted and too haggard to be desirable.

A knock at the door ended their whispers. Katherine grabbed her hand.

Camille inhaled a ragged breath. "That might be Mr. Dedeaux. Let me do the talking."

Katherine stood next to the chair and straightened her long auburn hair. Even in her brother's trousers and plain shirt, she was a beauty. Camille smiled at her sister's attempt to look brave. With a reassuring touch to her arm, Camille opened the door.

The guard stepped in, followed by a dark little man, slight in build with beady black eyes.

"This man says he has business with you and the major said to allow it." The guard stepped aside to let Mr. Dedeaux into the room.

"Camille. Katherine. Are you okay?" Mr. Dedeaux reached out and hugged Camille.

Camille savored the safety of his arms. "Thank you so much for coming. We didn't know the city had gotten dangerous, or we certainly wouldn't have come."

"Things have gone downhill with so many more troops in town, but I'm glad you came." He extended a crudely wrapped package to her. "It's fabric for your mother. I've hoarded it for you in the hopes you'd come again."

She took the package that had obviously been opened and hastily rewrapped by the guard. "We have a few pieces of clothing if you're interested, that is, what's left of them."

Camille leered at the guard. He smirked, but said nothing.

Concern creased Mr. Dedeaux's brow. "Did you run into trouble? Have these soldiers harmed you or your sister?"

"They ruined some of our merchandise, but we're okay."

She straightened her shoulders and turned to the dresser where the salvaged pieces lay displayed for him to examine.

He touched one small pink gown with rows of tiny tucks stitched around the bottom. "Oh, as usual, these things are exquisite." He looked up with admiration in his eyes. "We don't have much of a market these days, you know, but there are still a few wealthy families left in the city."

She detected a nervous quiver in Mr. Dedeaux's voice as he continued, "Some of the Yanks will buy little things to take home to their families when they leave here, I'm sure."

He picked up each piece and examined it carefully. "Such fine workmanship. You girls and your mother do magic with the needle. Just wonderful."

Camille tried to keep her voice calm as well. "Can you use them? We really need the money."

"Yes, yes. We can do business. He took out a piece of paper and did some calculations. He held the paper out for Camille to see the sum, but the guard immediately stepped away from the wall and grabbed the paper.

"It's only my offer," Mr. Dedeaux said meekly, stepping away from the guard.

The guard looked it over, grunted, then shoved it back into Mr. Dedeaux's now trembling hand. His voice was barely audible. "It's not much, but it's in good gold pieces that can be used anywhere."

In the past Camille would never have accepted such a low offer, but these weren't normal times. She swallowed the lump forming in her chest and nodded, knowing he was doing his best. "Of course, we accept your offer. Would you give me a hand repackaging these things? Katherine, you can help."

While they rewrapped the clothing and stacked the packages, the guard leaned against the door, bored.

Mr. Dedeaux glanced at the guard, then leaned closer to Camille. "I heard the Biloxi Rifles were near Vicksburg," he whispered. "Charles might be able to sneak off to see the family."

Camille squeezed her eyes and swallowed a wad

of emotion that tightened her chest. "Oh, how wonderful, but I won't say anything to Mother. I don't want to get her hopes up, but, oh God, I'll pray he can come home for a little while. It would do Mother so much good. I worry about her all the time."

She stopped and glanced at the guard, worried that at any minute he'd step behind her, crash his rifle into her head, then drag her away to the stockades.

He still rested against the door.

"I'll pray for your family as well," Mr. Dedeaux whispered, then in a louder voice added, "That ought to do it." He turned, then dropped a gold coin on the dresser. His voice was casual, but his face had paled and beads of sweat gathered across his brow. "You tell your mama how wonderful these gowns are and how much they'll be admired."

"Thank you, sir. Thank you for everything. I don't know if we'll be able to get into the city again, but after the war is over, we'll be back. These Yankees won't be here forever." She spoke loud enough for the guard to hear.

The guard smirked again. "Your time's up."

Mr. Dedeaux gave both girls a hug then lifted his packages. "Take care of yourself. Maybe I can get permission to travel to Biloxi to pick up merchandise, so tell your mother not to stop sewing. It's amazing what you can get permission to do if it helps those in charge."

Good-byes were said and the door closed behind the two men.

Camille leaned up against the dressing table with her back to it. Her body began to quiver.

"What's the matter, Camille? You're pale. What did Mr. Dedeaux say? Was it something good? Aren't you happy that we were able to sell some of the clothes?"

Camille nodded and kept the information about her brother to herself. "Of course, I'm happy. I'm just a little nervous over everything that's happened today. I guess my body is late in reacting."

Katherine stepped near her sister and hugged her. "I think you did just fine, Camille."

Camille hugged her sister back. The girls had only one gold coin, and no medicine to take back, but they had survived a nightmare in a city where they should not have been.

"You did just fine too, Katherine. Just fine."

The sucking black mud on the road had not dried for the return trip the next day. Camille sat next to her unusually quiet sister and seethed over the happenings that had taken place the day before. She'd never had negative contact with the Yankee army, but now she harbored a personal grudge against them.

She should be grateful for her and her sister's safety, but other things clouded her brain, things that would make their life more miserable than usual. Her blood boiled when she thought about the soldiers taking the salt. She and her two sisters and even some of her neighbors had worked so hard to gather it from the Gulf, but now they had nothing to show for their effort but leathery hands and empty pockets.

At least the handmade clothes had been salvaged, but her eyes burned with fury each time she thought about the mud stains on the delicate needlework.

Camille hadn't admitted it to the soldiers, but she and her sisters had helped her mother stitch the clothing, one of the few joys that she had left. Stitching the delicate fabric soothed her soul, took her mind away from the hurt and the misery of the war. At times she pretended her stitches adorned a new ball gown to dazzle a handsome beau or tiny garments for her firstborn. But they were all dreams.

"Stupid war!"

"What did you say, Camille?"

"Nothing. I guess I was just thinking out loud. Are you ready for a break? We could stop on the road and rest."

She really didn't want to stop even for a second, but Katherine's delicate features tugged at her heart.

Katherine shook her head. "No, let's keep going. I want to get home."

Camille acknowledged her answer with a smile, then shook Nancy's reins a little harder. Daylight was fading, and after the confrontation yesterday with the soldiers, she couldn't get home fast enough.

At daybreak the next morning she would start her nursing rounds with her mother or climb into a little skiff to fish for her family. Fishing had kept them alive. The peace and tranquility she found out on the water would be welcomed after her trip to New Orleans.

Even her stained fishing dress would feel better than the clothes she wore now. The small pitcher of water she and Katherine had been given at the boardinghouse hadn't been enough to take away the mud. Tomorrow in the boat she'd let her hair hang down and allow the sweet breeze to whip it around her face.

"Camille, do you think Charles will ever come home?" Katherine's question brought Camille out of her daydream.

She didn't want to talk about her brother and his absence, but her sister deserved an answer, and keeping the fact that he might be near wasn't fair.

"Of course we'll see him again." She patted her sister's leg and smiled. "Katherine, Mr. Dedeaux told me that he heard the Biloxi Rifles might be in Vicksburg."

Katherine's hands flew to her mouth. "Oh, that's wonderful. We're going to see Charles."

"Now, Katherine, don't get your hopes up. He might get home, but he might not. Vicksburg is a long way away."

"It's been so long since we've seen him. I just know he'll come for a visit."

"We'll pray that he does, but you can't let yourself be disappointed if he doesn't."

Katherine's voice dropped to an almost whisper. "I get scared sometimes, Camille. I'm so scared we won't ever see him again."

"Me too," Camille added, "but thinking the worst isn't doing anyone any good, especially around Mama. She's scared too. She doesn't say anything, but I've seen her sitting on the pier alone crying. She's worried about all of us, but especially about Charles."

"I know. I wish I knew what to say to her and to all the other mothers. I wish Father was here to help us."

"Yes, things would be easier for all of us if he hadn't died, but we can't bring him back either."

"But now Mama might have some hope with Charles nearby."

Camille prayed Katherine was right. There was so little to say to all the mothers whose sons were fighting in faraway fields. Life had been put on hold and those left behind could do nothing but wait and hope they could find enough food to keep their families alive.

For the rest of the afternoon, they rode in silence. Katherine leaned her head against Camille and slept. By sunset the crackling of the wheels on the oyster-shell roads announced their return to the little village north of Biloxi.

Mrs. Hollander was sitting in one of the big rockers on the front porch when they neared the house. Throwing aside her sewing, she ran to the fence to meet them.

A lump formed in Camille's throat when her mother

began to wave. Her prematurely gray hair was neatly pulled back in a small bun. The familiar cotton dress would be pressed and clean. Everything about her mother was meticulous, even the faded ribbons on her collar, a reminder of better times, but tied and worn proudly.

A wrinkled hand, looking older than it should, shaded her eyes from the setting sun that shot its last rays through the opening of the trees. Deep crevices marked her mother's brow with concern since she wasn't expecting them until tomorrow.

Camille fought back the urge to cry. They were coming home empty-handed, adding more weight to her mother's already stooped shoulders.

Camille finished unhitching the mare and headed toward the barn, leaving Katherine to relate the story to Dorothy, the middle sister, and to her mother. By the time she had watered and fed Nancy, Camille's rage had turned into a heavy sadness she hated even worse. Screaming with rage was better than feeling self-sorrow.

She slapped Nancy's rump lovingly. "Thanks for hanging in there, ole girl."

The screen door squeaked as she entered the house. She accepted a cup of water from her mother with a smile. "Thank you, Mama. It's all I want right now."

Her mother kissed her gently on her forehead. "I understand."

In her room, Camille poured water into a snowy white bowl and washed herself slowly and carefully. With each swipe of the cloth, she removed another layer of humiliation she and her sister had endured, and by the time the water in the bowl had turned the color of mud, she felt better.

Lying across her bed, she took a deep breath and tried not the think of how the family would manage.

Her mother opened the door with a quick knock and stepped in. "Are you really okay?"

"Yes, ma'am. My arm's a little sore from falling out of the wagon." She smiled at the sight she must have made. "But I guess except for that and hurt pride, I'm okay."

"Why don't you come in and get something to eat?"

Camille shook her head. "No, I just want to rest. I'm not hungry."

Mrs. Hollander rubbed her daughter's hair. "Whatever you want, but don't feel too bad about what happened. From what Katherine has said, your trip could've been a lot worse."

Camille nodded. Her mother kissed her on the top of the head. "I saw Michael today."

"How is he?" She and Michael had been raised together, and now he'd returned from the war missing a leg.

"Mr. Summers gave me a cup of liquor for some deserving young patient. I let Michael have a few sips to help with the pain. He smiled his thanks and then asked about you."

"I'll go with you on your next round. I worry so much about him."

Mrs. Hollander stood up and heaved a big breath. "We all do, but he's a strong young man with a future still ahead of him if he keeps his spirits up. He'll make some woman a good husband in spite of the fact that he'll have only one leg."

Camille accepted a kiss from her mother, but didn't comment about the prospects of Michael's future.

Her mother left with a smile on her face. She'd always encouraged Camille when it came to Michael, but in her heart Camille knew he could never be more than a friend.

When she was alone, Camille sat up on the side of the bed and picked up a silver-handled mirror. Given to her as payment for nursing a member of the family in one of the big beach manors, it was one of her few valuable possessions. The intricate details in the handle cooled her hand.

She examined her shoulder. Its clear reflection showed a slight bruise and a scrape, but she'd be okay. She worked the shoulder around, hoping that tomorrow she wouldn't be too sore to do her fishing.

She stared into the mirror. From spending her days out on the water, the sun had turned her milky white complexion to a golden brown. Secretly, the rich tone of her skin pleased her, but she was afraid none of the young men would think it flattering—that is, if any of the young men returned from the war.

Michael still wanted to hold her hand, but she hoped he only needed someone to help him get through the suffering.

Her gaze lowered to the floor as she remembered that none of the Union soldiers in New Orleans had looked at her in the way they'd looked at Katherine. The young men were drawn to Katherine's youth and delicate features, but not to her with her mud-splattered clothing and hair. She shuddered at the appearance she had presented.

But then she thought about the major. He had looked at her, really looked. She'd felt his stare all the way down to her toes.

Closing her eyes, she wrapped her arms around her body and relished the sensation of feeling like a woman, even if it had been an enemy officer who'd made her feel that way. She trembled at the remembrance of his direct stare, his tall statue and lean lines.

She blinked, embarrassed that she'd allowed him into her thoughts and pushed his image aside.

Sighing, she lowered the mirror to see the rest of her body. Father Murray wouldn't approve of her doing it, but she had to make sure she hadn't started wrinkling like the older women in the community. She was over twenty, she reminded herself, and that was getting old.

Her legs were still firm and smooth, and she'd lost her little pudgy stomach. Before the war she'd always had to squeeze into a waist cincher to wear her ball gowns. Now the only things that covered her body were faded dresses and her brother's left-behind trousers.

Carefully, she placed the mirror on the dresser. In spite of the disastrous last two days, sleep would come easy that night. Home and safe, she refused to think any more about the stolen salt, the ruined garments, or even the officer that had made her so furious.

That night, in her own bed, she didn't fight the exhaustion that burned her muscles and scattered her thoughts. With her sisters safely in their own room and her mother out on the porch in the moonlight, she welcomed sleep.

In her dreams she would wear beautiful gowns and dance with young men who saw her as the young girl she was before the war.

So what if some of her suitors looked like a major on a tall black horse? They were dreams and nothing more.

The young men could appear any way she liked.

Chapter Three

Jake stretched his long legs and tried to find a little room to spread out in the small, open boat. Two months had passed since his trip to New Orleans, and even though he was on a mission to track down a band of marauders hiding out in the bayous, he had a one-day reprieve. Today he headed to the Darcey estate to spend a relaxing evening as a real human being. No sand. No soldiers waiting for him to voice a command. No prisoners.

Just real, home-cooked food and a big porch where he planned to find his soul again, if that was possible.

On the island the oppressive heat beat down relentlessly on his men as well as on the prisoners, and this was only June. A hint of guilt nipped at his heart for getting away, but he'd gladly accepted Mrs. Darcey's invitation. Packing his best uniform, his spirits lifted for the first time in weeks. He stepped lightly through his last few checks on the island, gave final orders, and even found himself humming as he swatted the remaining grains of sand that clung to his baggage. The invitation had been a blessing.

Now as the small boat labored through the choppy water, he found himself wondering who would be at the Darceys'. On other occasions, their niece Mary Elizabeth from Mobile had been there. A gorgeous girl with a beauty rarely matched in his hometown, she came from a well-to-do family, old money as it was referred to down here.

Her delicate features, genteel Southern manners, and a sense of perfection stayed with him for days after he parted from her. Usually they'd dance in the parlor to the music of the piano, then enjoy the balmy Southern nights out on the big veranda surrounded by her family and friends.

Nothing had ever happened between them, but Jake felt sure had he made the move, she wouldn't have objected. He was an officer in the Union Army, and he had enough sense not to get involved with the daughter of an old Southern family.

It didn't keep him from enjoying her company, though, and as uncomfortable as the boat ride was today, he wasn't complaining. He would enjoy the distraction.

As his boat neared the shore, it was impossible for

him not to also think about another woman. The memory of Camille Hollander had played with his mind ever since he'd seen her in New Orleans several months ago.

Camille and Mary Elizabeth were as far removed from each other as the North was from the South. Mary Elizabeth would never have ventured out to New Orleans to trade salt and clothing to help her people.

Camille was cut from a different bolt than Mary Elizabeth. The vision of Camille standing in the middle of the road shaking the mud from the clothes had stuck with him, woke him in the middle of the night, and flooded his thoughts when he walked the island alone.

Camille had burned an impression on his brain that would be hard to shake. As she stood her ground against him and the men on the road, he knew there was nothing coarse about her, only a haunting beauty he'd felt in the brief meeting as their paths had crossed.

Closing his eyes, he allowed a vision of her to soothe his mind and before he knew it, Sergeant Maxwell Stafford was touching his arm. "Major, we're almost to the Darcey dock."

Jake's eyes flew open. "Thank you, Stafford. The ride was so smooth it put me to sleep." The young sergeant laughed at his lie.

Joseph, a slave who had been given his freedom but chose to stay at the Darcey home, stood at the end of the pier waiting to give assistance with the ropes. He waved.

"Welcome, Major Warren. Welcome."

Jake waved back and smiled. "Thank you, Joseph. Believe me, it's a pleasure to be here." Jake had liked and respected Joseph from his first visit.

Jake threw him his bag then turned to Sergeant Stafford. "Take the men to Biloxi and bivouac along front beach after your routine patrol. You can pick me up tomorrow afternoon about three. I'm sure the Darceys will have something for the men to eat."

He jumped onto the pier. Immediately the cool breeze blowing in off the bay and the refreshing shade from the enormous oak trees made him feel like a new man.

He followed Joseph down the pier and across the lawn. Mrs. Darcey got up from a huge rocker on the front porch to greet him.

"Major Warren, I'm so glad you could make it." She extended her hand in greeting as Jake stepped onto the porch.

"I'm honored to be here, ma'am. You can't imagine what a relief it is to get off that island for a couple of days." Bending down, he kissed her hand.

The lady seemed to be thinner than the last time he'd visited, and the dress she wore was the same one she had worn on his last visit, but she held her head high. War took away from everyone, though as he looked around, he couldn't help but notice that some definitely fared better than others. The Darceys were making the best of a horrible situation. They coped by befriending the men in blue, and he certainly wasn't dumb enough to not take advantage of their hospitality.

He'd found that as the war progressed, a shortage of food was leading to starvation as the few villagers waited in a sort of no-man's-land for the war to resolve itself away from their shore.

The soldiers on the island traded coffee and tea and anything else they could spare for chickens, eggs, and salt. It was a mutual agreement among most of the residents and the soldiers. No one wanted to do harm to those who were left.

Thinking about trading salt brought to mind Camille and her sister. A deep sorrow still hurt each time he remembered having to confiscate the salt they wanted to trade.

Mrs. Darcey fanned herself and interrupted his thoughts of the women on the road. "As I said in my note to you, we really have nothing special planned for the weekend. My niece, Mary Elizabeth, and her mother are coming in at any moment. I thought how delightful it would be if you could be here. We've scraped together a few little extra treats. We all need a break in these times."

"You're so right. How is Mr. Darcey?"

"I'm really worried about my husband. He's taken to his bed again. In fact, I'm considering sending Joseph across the bay to get someone to come look at him."

A young black girl came out carrying a pitcher of lemonade and some glasses, set them on the small round table, then left without saying a word.

As Jake sat in one of the enormous rockers, Mrs. Darcey poured them each a glass.

"This is a real treat. We haven't had real lemonade in so long," she said. "While Joseph was in Mobile last week he ran into one of the plantation workers from Florida. He managed to get a few lemons for us. He actually had to hide them under the seat of the wagon to get them out of the city. I've been waiting to share them with you and dear Mary Elizabeth."

Jake's first sip tingled his taste buds. "Thank you. You can't imagine how refreshing this is. I think I taste real sugar. Now that is really a luxury."

Mrs. Darcey fluttered her eyelids as she nodded her pleasure at his appreciation of her drink. "Your uniform looks damp. Was the trip from the island very rough?"

"Oh, no, not at all. It's always a little choppy, but except for the heat of the sun, it was a perfect day for a boat ride. If we could figure a way to get some shade on these blasted open boats, we'd be a whole lot better off."

"Why don't you take your glass of lemonade and go on to your cottage? I'm sure you'd like to change or at least rest before our company arrives."

"I'm looking forward to seeing everyone." At that he got up, excused himself, then made his way to the cottage.

The little white guest cottage nestled under a huge oak couldn't have looked any better had it been the Grand Royale Hotel back home. Jake looked forward to the cool breeze blowing in from the windows that overlooked the west side of the bay. Tiny, but immaculately clean, the cottage would feel like a bit of luxury with its soft featherbed and crisp, clean sheets. Even now, the gravel under his boots sounded good as he walked down the winding path lined with welltrimmed shrubs.

Thinking about his men camping along the rocky shore fighting the mosquitoes sent another wave of guilt up his spine, but he reassured himself that the southern breeze coming in off the sound would keep them cool as well and maybe some of the local families would bring them food. Hanging onto that last thought, he stepped inside the cottage.

Joseph had already carried his bag inside and hung his uniform and shirt. A fresh pitcher of water waited for him on the stand. He wasted no time in stripping off his wet shirt and using the water to cool his body and remove the salt. In no time, he stretched out on the bed and let his mind ramble from one insignificant topic to the next until he drifted off to sleep.

After a late supper of fresh vegetables and platters of several kinds of fish, Jake leaned back in his chair. "This was the best meal I've had since I was last here.

I won't even ask how you managed to get all of these vegetables, and I certainly won't tell my cook what I ate."

"Oh, dear, you do know how to flatter a lady," said Mrs. Darcey. "Joseph knows everyone around here and has connections up and down the coast. He even knows servants from New Orleans who manage to sneak over food. He's been a lifesaver, especially since Mr. Darcey's health has been so delicate lately."

Mary Elizabeth, who had been toying with the food on her plate, spoke up. "I just hate that Uncle couldn't come down tonight."

"He sends his love and says for you to come up tomorrow morning to see him. Why don't we move to the cool of the porch? That is, if you've had your fill."

Jake laughed and stood up. "I think I've had my fill and enough for several others." He helped Mrs. Darcey with her chair then stepped over to Mary Elizabeth's.

As she stood, Mary Elizabeth placed a hand on Jake's arm. "If all Yankees were as kind as you, Major Warren, we'd not be fighting this awful war."

Jake smiled, but couldn't come up with an answer that wouldn't make her statement seem ridiculous so he simply let her take his arm, then escorted her out onto the porch.

Mrs. Darcey sat in a high-back rocker near the end of the porch, but spoke in a loud enough voice for

Jake to hear. "I left instructions to have the leftovers packaged up to give to your men tomorrow when they come back for you."

"Thank you. That will help ease my guilt for enjoying this lovely evening with you ladies."

Jake seated Mary Elizabeth on a lounge chair, looked around for an empty chair elsewhere, but finding none, sat next to her.

"How long will you be here, Major?"

"Unfortunately my men and I are on the mainland on a mission. They'll pick me up tomorrow. I'm lucky to be able to get away for one night. You can't imagine how I look forward to staying in the cottage away from the sand and heat. It's amazing how one appreciates little things in times like these."

Mary Elizabeth sighed. "I know exactly how you feel. I'd give anything for a new ball dress or even for a ball to attend."

Jake noticed that nothing was wrong with the dress she had on, especially when he remembered the clothes that Camille had been wearing on the road to New Orleans.

He frowned, wondering why he had thought about the other girl while surrounded by these ladies.

Mary Elizabeth hadn't noticed. "We've tried to keep up our lifestyle the best we could after the war began." Her bottom lip pouted and her fingers twisted a ribbon on her dress, reminding Jake of someone recanting a tragic story. He fought to hide a grin.

"We even tried giving several parties at the beginning," she continued, "but there were no men to invite. I was just sick about the whole thing. I think it's a shame that all the young men were sent away."

Jake didn't comment. What could he add to such a selfish remark?

Mary Elizabeth continued to ramble on about insignificant social happenings in Mobile, but Jake's mind tuned her in and out at will. Unlike his previous visits, today the girl's whining grated on his nerves.

The dusk of the day was his favorite, and at the moment he wished he could sit alone and enjoy the wonderful shade and quiet evening.

"Are you listening, Major Warren?"

Jake looked up to see that Mary Elizabeth looked perturbed. "I'm sorry. I guess I'm a bit tired. My mind slipped off into nothingness for a minute. What did you say?"

"I asked if you were going to stay in the South after this dreadful war is over."

"No, I'll probably go back to Rhode Island. My father has a bank, and I'm sure he's ready for me to take over. I never really wanted to, but after all of this, I think it might be nice. Or maybe I'll stay in the military or get into politics. Who knows what the future holds for any of us."

"Oh, you should spend some time with us. I'm sure you would love Mobile when none of this ugliness is going on."

"I'm sure it's a most wonderful city, but sometimes it's nice to be around your family and old friends." He stood up and stretched. "I hope you don't mind, but like I said, I'm rather tired, and I think I'll retire early. Tomorrow my men and I have the unpleasant task of venturing into the bayou for some deserters."

Mary Elizabeth placed her hand over her heart. "Oh, that sounds just dreadful—and dangerous."

"We hope it won't be dreadful or dangerous. We have some good information about where the group might be so we think we can surround them without much fighting."

Mrs. Darcey spoke up. "Well, I for one want those nasty men captured. They've scared just about everyone around here and have stolen from all of us."

"We'll do our best, Mrs. Darcey." He turned to Mary Elizabeth, took her hand, and kissed it gently on the back. "You have lovely hands. In fact, you're a lovely young lady. I'm sure your memory is getting some man through the days he has to spend in the fields."

"You're too kind, sir. I have no special beau."

"That's a shame. The young men of Mobile just don't know what they've let slip by them." He turned to Mrs. Darcey and Mary Elizabeth's mother. "It was a lovely evening, but if you don't mind, I'm going to say good night."

The food and the visit had been nice, but not as inviting as his cool cottage. After stripping his shirt, he pulled the solitary chair to the window where every sparkle of the moon and the stars on the water seemed to be within arm's reach. Lighting a cigar, he leaned back in his chair and relaxed. If his men knew he'd left a beautiful lady to sit alone in his cottage, they'd accuse him of being insane. It didn't matter. Tonight he chose solitude.

Resting his elbows on the windowsill, he flicked his cigar ashes into the yard. A light flickered in the distance along the shoreline and his thoughts immediately turned to Camille. Her home was somewhere in this area. He wondered if it could be near the Darceys'.

After spending the evening listening to Mary Elizabeth's superficial topics, he longed to sit alone with someone like Camille. As little as he knew of her, he guessed her viewpoints on the war had to be more interesting than Mary Elizabeth's.

Jake grinned. Mary Elizabeth would need smelling salts if anyone put her in Camille's situation. Camille was strong, but to most in the South, being a strong woman was not desirable. To him it was admirable. None of the women here tonight were like her, and he felt sure that when the war ended, it would be women like Camille who would be able to cope with the changes that would come to the state.

And changes would come. The South was losing, and after being among the people here for so long, he felt a deep sorrow for them. Some of them who thrived on a pampered life would not be able to handle their future.

Camille and others like her would.

Camille wrinkled her nose at the dirty dishpan of water, picked it up, and marched out the back door. Even if their supply of lye soap was running low, she couldn't stand to use the water for more than a day or so. She'd rather wash her dishes in the bay water than with used soapy water.

After attending her mother on a few medical rounds in the early morning, Camille planned to help her sisters with the salt barrels while her mother looked in on several other men on the other side of the bay. Being outside with her two sisters on such a beautiful morning would be a welcome relief, even if it meant tending salt barrels.

While tossing the dish water off the porch, she watched an old man pull his skiff up to their pier. It took a moment to recognize the Darcey servant. She waved her hands and walked down to the water's edge to meet him.

"What're you doing in this neighborhood? Come up to the porch and I'll get you a glass of water."

"No, ma'am, that's okay. I've got to hurry back. Mrs. Darcey sent me to speak to your mama."

"Is someone sick?"

"Yessum. Mr. Darcey is down again ailing and she

wants your mama to come over and give him some of that tonic like she done the last time."

"My mother's gone into Biloxi, and she's planning to stay over until tomorrow. Can I help? I do rounds with her all the time. I know what she gave to Mr. Darcey."

Joseph's expression went blank. Servants weren't used to making that kind of decision. He stood silently for several minutes staring at the weeds growing around the steps.

Finally Camille answered for him. "You wait right here. I'll go with you and take the tonic, and we'll let Mrs. Darcey decide if I should look in on her husband."

That seemed to satisfy Joseph. He smiled.

Camille went inside alone. Checking to make sure she had her mother's homemade tonic in her bag, she snapped it shut, then pulled her hair back with a faded ribbon, but one that wasn't frayed. For a moment she thought about changing into her one "Sunday dress" but decided against it. She was going to the Darceys' to help a patient, not to show off. If the man was ill, no one but Mrs. Darcey would be there anyway. Why should she try to impress her?

Her sisters followed her to the boat with Camille giving them simple reminders all the way.

"Should you go without Mama knowing?" Dorothy, the worrier in the family, touched her arm.

"It'll be okay. I won't get to help you at the barrels today, but maybe tomorrow." She kissed her sisters, then waved as Joseph pushed away from the pier.

The small boat glided across the bay, making the trip much too short for Camille, who relaxed while Joseph rowed. He was old, but he had not lost the strength in his arms. It wasn't often that someone else did the rowing when Camille was in a boat. She raised her face to the midmorning sun and closed her eyes. Even in wartime, some things were still wonderful.

The side door to the stately home swung open and Mrs. Darcey stepped out as soon as the boat reached the pier. Even from the pier Camille could see she was dressed for company today with her soft blue day dress and tightly curled hair.

Camille wished she'd worn her other dress. She tried to straighten her own windblown tresses but was certain that they fought to escape the tiny ribbon that held them captive. Giving up, she picked up her medical bag and followed Joseph up the dock to greet Mrs. Darcey.

"I saw the boat from the window in the parlor. Come in, dear."

Camille greeted her with a smile. In spite of the fact that she lived in a style far beyond the Hollander family, Mrs. Darcey had always been a favorite to Camille. While the Darceys made their fortune in sugarcane, the Hollanders gained their respect in the community from their medical service. Camille's mother and now Camille continued Dr. Hollander's service after his boating death.

No fortunes were made by his years of dedication, but the respect they gained made Camille proud of the Hollander name.

"Mama is in Biloxi," Camille said as Mrs. Darcey took her by the arm and led her to the wide steps leading up to the front porch. "I came in her place. I brought the same tonic that she gave to Mr. Darcey before."

"Thank you so much. I'm so glad you came, Camille. I'm sure you'll be able to see to his needs until your mama can come." She opened the ornate mahogany door. "Would you like a glass of lemonade before you go in to see him?"

Camille's taste buds danced at the mention of the drink, but she chose to wait. "No, thank you, not now. Maybe after I check on Mr. Darcey."

"Certainly. Alice is with him in the upstairs bedroom. If you need anything, send the girl for me. I'll be in the parlor. Would you meet me there afterward? I'll have you a glass poured."

Camille found her way to the bedroom. Sunshine poured in from large windows overlooking the water and reflected on the hardwood floor. Camille wondered how they remained so beautiful in wartime, but immediately reminded herself not to compare. Mrs. Darcey's former slaves continued to keep up the house with the few resources available.

The Hollander house, though spotlessly clean, showed signs of neglect. How could the girls and her mother wax and polish floors and keep the yard trimmed when salt barrels needed tending and fish had to be caught to keep alive?

With a silent reprimand for wanting her old life back, Camille closed the door behind her. Mr. Darcey lay in a huge bed, unmoving, with Alice fanning him with a large oriental-style fan. She stepped away from the bed when Camille entered the room.

Camille smiled at Alice, but spoke to Mr. Darcey. "Hello, Mr. Darcey. I've brought you some of Mama's tonic."

Opening his eyes slightly at her voice, he grinned and nodded. Camille poured him several large spoonfuls, then rearranged his pillows. She washed his forehead and the two of them talked quietly. With no fever, Camille credited his age, the heat, and the war in general for his condition. Even though the Darceys didn't feel the hardships of wartime as severely as most of the other coast families, she knew it had not been easy for them.

Finally, the elderly man drifted off to sleep and she left the room quietly. Straightening her dress and her hair once more, she followed Alice to the door of the parlor. She wanted to feel guilty about accepting the lemonade while her sisters worked the salt barrels, but nothing happened. She'd accept it as payment for bringing over the tonic.

As Alice opened the door to the parlor, Camille's enthusiasm for the lemonade vanished. At least four or five other people sat or stood around the room.

Mrs. Darcey met her at the door and took her by the arm. "Come right in, Camille."

Camille didn't look around the room but spoke directly to her. "I gave your husband his tonic, and I feel confident he doesn't have any disease. I think he needs a good rest. Mama will be home tomorrow, and I'll tell her to come over."

Her eyes remained fixed on Mrs. Darcey, but all the time she was conscious of the presence of other people. From the corner of her eye, crisp pastel told her several ladies stood near the fireplace. From the tinkling of crystal she knew they too were enjoying refreshing lemonade or brandy and doing what richer, more affluent families did at morning gatherings.

"I'd like you to meet some of my friends, Camille. Several of our neighbors from the beachfront joined us this morning."

Camille groaned inwardly, but kept her head held high and her shoulders back.

Mrs. Darcey looped her arm through Camille's for the introductions. "This is my sister from Mobile and her daughter, Mary Elizabeth. I think you two young ladies have met before."

Camille touched the older lady's hand in greeting, then smiled at Mary Elizabeth.

"Camille. You remember me, don't you? I was on

the swing one day when you stopped in to bring Auntie some fish." Her words dripped in honey and condescension.

Camille smiled and swallowed the urge to slap. "Oh, yes, I do remember, Mary Elizabeth. You were complaining how hot it was to the young soldier who shared the swing with you."

Camille followed the tug of Mrs. Darcey's arm. "This is Mr. and Mrs. Mallory. You know them from down the waterfront."

Camille nodded.

"How do you do, Camille? Mrs. Darcey's been telling us how much of a godsend you and your mother have been to the locals. Thankfully, we've been fortunate enough not to need the services of your medical skills." She laughed delicately and fanned herself. "I certainly hope it stays that way."

"And this, Camille, is Major Jake Warren . . ." but the rest of her words faded. There, now leaning against the door that Camille had entered, was the officer from New Orleans. Humiliation flooded over her. She didn't want to ever see him again. Not like this. Not wearing her faded fishing dress, when the last time he'd seen her, she had mud splattered over her entire body. She wasn't much better today.

Enraged at herself for feeling embarrassed, she threw her shoulders back and reached out a hand to him.

"How do you do, Camille? It's nice to see you

again." His voice, as mellow and as deep as before, stabbed at her heart.

"Oh, do you know each other?" asked Mrs. Darcey.

Camille pulled her hand to her body and spoke up. "Yes, we've had occasion to meet, but I wouldn't say that we know each other."

"I'm glad to see that you've recovered nicely," he said.

Infuriated that he dared to mention her incident with the troops on the road, she wanted to scream, but instead she nodded. "Thank you, sir. I have."

Camille turned to Mrs. Darcey, who looked confused. Giving thanks that she was much too ladylike to ask about her incident, Camille found her voice.

"I must be going now. My sisters are home alone, and I promised them I'd return before dark. I've left your husband's tonic with Alice and have instructed her to give him some again in the morning. As I said earlier, I'll have Mama come over when she returns."

"Please stay and have that glass of lemonade before you rush off."

Camille couldn't believe she was refusing the chance to have lemonade, but the room felt as though it were closing in on her. "No, no, I don't think I'd care for any."

Camille said her good-byes graciously to the ladies and men in the room, then faced Jake. "Good-bye, Major Warren. I'm sure you'll enjoy your visit here."

With a quick turn she was out the door and flying

across the lawn to the safety of the boat. Her heart beat wildly. Her palms were sticky from sweat.

At the boat dock, she slumped against a piling and inhaled deeply to clear her head. Her simple house call had turned into a nightmare. She closed her eyes and mumbled curses for the man in the blue uniform that made her feel—well, she wasn't sure how she felt, but it wasn't right.

Joseph waited for her to straighten up, then helped her into the boat, but instead of getting in, he stepped back. Major Warren stepped around him.

"Camille, wait. I hope you don't mind that I followed you down here."

Camille gave a start as Major Warren's voice jolted her out of her mental ranting.

"I didn't mean to alarm you." Jake squatted down at the edge of the pier towering over Camille. "I wanted to say a few words to you, and I didn't feel comfortable surrounded by all those other people. Here." He stretched out his hand and handed her a glass of lemonade.

Camille stared.

"Would you stop being so stubborn and take it? It's too hot a day to turn down such a luxury."

His smile melted her resistance. Hating the way he made her feel was one thing, but refusing that glass was just being stupid. She took it. "Thank you."

"I was wondering how you were doing?"

She tried to be prim and proper as she knew Mary

Elizabeth must have been. "I'm doing fine. My sisters and mother and I are managing."

She sipped the lemonade, but with Jake hovering over her, she couldn't taste a thing.

"I wanted you to know how sorry I was that we couldn't come to terms with the salt and medicines. I had my orders. I didn't have an option. I hope you understood."

Camille lifted her gaze to him. "I guess I would've done the same in a similar situation. Still, coming home nearly empty-handed hurt a lot of people. We needed that medicine." Her voice softened. "This war seems like a horrible dream."

The words slipped from her mouth before she realized what she'd said. Why had she admitted such a thing to a Yankee officer?

Major Warren let out a long breath. "Yes, there're horrors everywhere in war. I know that everyone down here along this coast is not as fortunate as the Darceys. They're an exception."

Now it was Camille's turn to be surprised. It was as though this Union officer understood how she and her fellow villagers suffered from lack of food and medicine.

"You're very observant, Major Warren. You're right, the Darceys have found a way to maintain a semblance of their old life, and none of us resent them for it at all. They're very generous people and try to help others the best way they can."

"That's good to know, and I have to tell you that Mrs. Darcey has great respect for what you and your mother do for the community."

Humiliation flooded Camille once more knowing that she had been the topic of conversation for these people.

An awkward silence fell over them. Camille finally lifted the glass to her lips and sipped the cool liquid.

Jake stood up as Joseph shuffled his feet. "Well, I just wanted to check on you," Jake said.

Camille held out the empty glass. "Thank you for bringing this out to me. It really was special."

His fingers brushed hers as his hand wrapped around the glass. Camille's heart pounded against her chest. Not since being jostled around by the soldiers on the road had it gotten such a workout, but this time it wasn't from fear. She jerked her hand away.

He nodded and smiled. "Yes, very special."

The heavy air in her bedroom stuck to her body even though she had both of her windows open and her thin gown pulled up all the way to her hips. Miserably, Camille lay in her bed thinking about the afternoon.

Why had she gotten so touchy lately? Why had she been embarrassed at the Darcey home? Many times she and her mother had been introduced to the Darcey guests, and she had met each one with the pride that helping others brings. Their medical skills, as simple and homespun as they were, were all that the little village had, and she was proud of doing her part.

Today had been different. Today, she had been conscious of her dress, conscious of her windblown hair, and afraid of what those people thought of her. No, she corrected her line of thought. She was concerned about how Major Warren saw her among the other ladies in their fine attire.

"Oh, pooh," she said aloud, then hit the pillow. "This is nonsense. What difference does it make what he thinks of me?"

Squeezing her eyes shut, she tried to ignore the sticky night. She tossed and turned, then finally sat up on the side of the bed. The air was heavy, but it wasn't her physical discomfort that was keeping her awake. It was the discomfort she felt remembering the major standing in the same room with Mary Elizabeth.

"Just let him have her kind." She spoke out loud again, then walked over to the window. "I never want to see him again." The little lie made her feel better.

The moon reflected on the water, and for a moment she let herself imagine sitting on her own porch with a young man, but try as she might to envision sitting with some of the returning soldiers around the coast, or maybe even with Michael, she just couldn't. They all ended up looking like Jake Warren.

And she knew why. Just once, she'd like to meet him on equal terms. He made her feel something that no male had ever made her feel before, something she had suppressed for so long that she ached thinking about it.

She wanted a man to hold her, to dance with her, to make her feel feminine. She wanted Jake Warren if only for one night. But that would never be. Jake Warren was the enemy in this war. No matter if he socialized with the Darceys and had saved her life, he was untouchable.

Camille sighed, then turned and headed back to her bed.

Untouchable, maybe, but on this night when the air was as heavy as her heart, nothing kept her from dreaming of his arms around her.

Chapter Four

The hot days of summer slipped into even hotter and muggier days of September. More and more young men returned from the war, crippled and heartsick. No one spoke of the apparent hopeless effort of the South, but Camille saw it on all the faces she met. It showed in the eyes of the soldiers and could be read between the lines of the few letters that made it to scattered families. Anyone receiving a letter shared it with friends.

In the middle of September such a letter made its way to the Schmidts and was passed on to Mr. DeLaney, who hobbled down the road early one morning shouting and waving the letter.

Katherine and Dorothy saw him first. "Mama,

Mama, come quick. It's a letter. It has to be from Charles!"

Camille ran through the front door and out onto the porch. Mr. DeLaney, still waving the letter in front of him, stood out-of-breath at the foot of the stairs.

"It's from Charles, Camille. Where's your mama?"

In answer, Mrs. Hollander flew through the front door. "Oh, Bradley, is it really from Charles?" She reached out for it, then held it to her breast. Tears rolled down her cheeks.

"Mr. Schmidt brought it to me this morning. His son was brought in yesterday." Obviously exhausted from his trek down the road, he rested both hands on his knees. "Young Schmidt was wounded at Port Gibson. Charles was there too. He was there, Virginia! Do you know how close that is?"

"Open it, Mama. Open it!" Katherine begged.

Nodding through tears, she walked to the porch and sat down.

Camille held the two girls back. "Give her a minute. She's waited so long. We can wait a little longer."

She forced her attention away from the letter and looked down at Mr. DeLaney, gulping air and fanning himself. "Would you like something to drink, Mr. DeLaney?"

"No, I'll let you girls go to your mother and hear what Charles has to say. I'm sure she'll bring it on over for us to see soon enough."

Eager to hear what was in the letter, Camille said a

quick good-bye, then put her arm around Katherine's shoulder, waiting for her mother to give the word. Mrs. Hollander sat on the top step with the letter in her hand, a tiny quiver shaking the pages.

"Oh, girls, your brother's well. He hasn't even been wounded. He was just fine when he wrote this." With tears streaming down her face, she handed the one page, soiled and crumpled, to Camille.

Closing her eyes, Camille held it close to her face. Smells of battle clung to the pages: sweat, gunpowder, and the smell of fear. Maybe she imagined the odors. Maybe her senses heightened to feel nearer to Charles, but whatever it was, he was with her at that moment.

She swallowed her tears and read out loud.

Charles had been in Port Gibson when he wrote the letter. He wanted to get home for a visit, but having been made captain was making it hard for him to get away. Camille read it over and over to the girls. A weight had been lifted momentarily. The letter was over two weeks old, but at least they knew that two weeks ago, Charles had been alive and relatively close to home.

Dorothy stood up and looked down the shell road. "Mama, he might get here at any time. He could be on his way now."

Mrs. Hollander put her arm around her middle daughter. "Maybe he is, but let's not put too much hope in it."

"I know." Dorothy looked at Camille for reassurance.

"Maybe he is, Mama. Dorothy could be right, you know. I think we ought to get the house clean and try to find some sugar or something special if he does come in."

The next few days found the girls and Mrs. Hollander cleaning and flitting around the house and the yard as they hadn't done in a long time. All of them knew the chance that Charles could get away for a visit was slim, but no one actually said the words.

Another week went by with no word from Charles. The house had been cleaned and the yard around the house clipped and raked. Always, one of the girls sat on the front porch—just in case. Neighbors dropped in more frequently and sat with them, but Charles never showed up.

October's cooler evenings settled over the coastal villages with welcomed relief. The watch on the porch for Charles had been abandoned gradually, but the hope remained.

One afternoon as Camille sat on the pier trying to mend a hole in one of her few remaining crab traps, she watched a small open boat coming in from the south. Any strange boat in their waters sent a wave of panic through her. Holding her net still, she watched the boat until she recognized it as one from the island. She put down her net and waited.

Why was it heading to her pier? Would Major Warren be on the boat? She hadn't heard or seen him since the encounter at the Darceys', but with the possibility of his being on the boat, another moment of panic shot through her. She pinched her cheeks and straightened her skirt.

The boat with three men in Union uniforms pulled up alongside the pier. One of them stood up as he tossed Camille a line. "Good day, ma'am. Is this the Hollander home?"

Major Warren wasn't one of the men. Disappointment surprised her, but she plastered a smile for the men in the boat. "Yes, I'm Miss Hollander. What can I do for you?"

Camille's insides tightened.

"I'm Sergeant Maxwell Stafford. We have news to share with your family. Is Mrs. Hollander home?"

"I'll get her," Katherine spoke up and ran toward the house.

"If you'll tie the boat, you can come up to the house and we'll find something for you and your men to drink."

They followed, whispering as they followed her. She knew something was terribly wrong for them to have rowed all the way from the island. Sergeant Stafford looked nervous, the lines on his face much too deep for such a young man. Curiosity threatened to make her forget her manners.

Mrs. Hollander met on the porch. "What can I do for you men?"

Camille recognized the fear in her voice, but her mother stood straight and tall to hear whatever the men had to say. Katherine and Dorothy stood next to her. She pulled them close.

Sergeant Stafford took one step up on the porch, then stopped. "The news is both good and bad," he said. "I really don't know how to start." He looked at Camille for help, but without having any idea of what he was trying to say, she couldn't offer any assistance.

He looked back at Mrs. Hollander. "You know," he started and stammered, "Ship Island has been turned into a prisoner-of-war camp. Just this month we got about a thousand prisoners from several places along the Mississippi River and Louisiana."

"Charles," Camille said under her breath. From her side she heard her mother inhale deeply.

The young sergeant nodded. "That's what I came to tell you. Captain Hollander was taken a prisoner near Jackson, and he arrived with our first men last week via New Orleans."

"Last week?" Mrs. Hollander said.

"With so many men, it took us a good bit of time to process all of them. Major Warren called me in just this morning to tell me he was here and to come tell your family immediately."

Camille's head spun. Her stomach knotted. "Charles

is on the island? He's a prisoner?" Her sisters were saying something, but their words jumbled and made no sense to her.

"Is he wounded? Is he sick?"

"He's fine. He wasn't wounded at all."

"Oh, thank God."

Her mother reached out and placed a hand on the sergeant's arm. "Can we go out to see him?"

"Major Warren doesn't usually let family members visit the island and he certainly doesn't want you out there over night, but since your son is an officer and you're so close, he made an exception."

Mrs. Hollander grabbed the sergeant's arm. "So you're saying we can see him?"

"Yes, but not until tomorrow so we can go and return in one day and still give you a little time to visit." He and the other men stood up. "We have orders to stay on the other side of the bay tonight, but we'll be by just after daybreak to get you. If you'd like, you can take blankets, pillows, or anything that might make his stay more comfortable. We were sent prisoners, but not many supplies. The prisoners could use food too. Anything would be appreciated."

Camille and her mother shook the soldiers' hands, then walked with them down to the water's edge.

Joy at the thought of seeing her brother again pushed aside the pain of knowing he was being held a prisoner on a barren strip of land in the Gulf of Mexico just twelve miles from his home.

Once again their world had been turned upside down.

The next morning, long before daylight, the girls and Mrs. Hollander sat on the porch waiting for the boat. On the floor sat baskets of food and bundles of blankets and clothing. Food was scarce, but Mrs. Hollander managed to bake a pear pie. Dorothy and Katherine scurried from house to house until almost all the ingredients were donated. Those that couldn't be found were simply left out.

Word spread fast. Everyone living within hearing distance donated something that could be taken to their boys on the island.

Camille's heart leaped at the sight of the open boat materializing in the misty haze. They grabbed their packages and hurried to the pier to meet the boat.

Words were at a minimum as the boat pulled away. Each Hollander sat huddled next to the other deep in thought as the boat maneuvered between the two peninsulas. From there it skimmed westward around the end of Deer Island, and then southward toward the island that separated the Gulf from the Mississippi Sound, the island where Charles was being held.

Camille pulled her shawl tighter around her shoulders. It protected against the chill, but did very little against the spray from the waves.

Camille looked down at her Sunday dress, as she liked to call it. Even though October was the wrong season for the delicate spring green, it was the only decent dress that still fit. She felt good in it, better than she had in a long time. She wanted to look good for Charles, and in the back of her mind, she knew that Major Warren would see them. If he did, she wanted to be at her best—for once. If he could see her just once dressed as a lady, then her mind would be at rest and she wouldn't have to think about him again.

The eastern sky gradually turned from a pink to a streaked orange before the sun peeked over the horizon. Camille hummed a tune to herself, and before long, all the girls were humming. Turning from his oars, Sergeant Stafford smiled and rowed a little faster.

The miles between them and the island slowly decreased. The waters of the Sound turned from dull gray to blue, then to a sparkling blue-green. It was clean and clear and inviting. The trees at the eastern end of the island appeared, then gradually the white sands of the barren western end also took shape with one ominous structure jutting up into the horizon. She watched it materialize.

She'd heard stories of the fort that stood higher than the tallest beachfront home. Excitement and sadness descended on her shoulders. Charles was there as a prisoner.

Camille strained to see the other structures sprinkled along the tip of the island along with the massive round fort.

"Look at all the buildings," she heard her mother say.

"We've just built a lot of them, about forty in all," volunteered Private Martin. "In fact, some are still under construction. Like Sergeant Stafford said yesterday, we weren't expecting so many prisoners all at one time. Our prisoner stockade isn't finished. One of the buildings is ready, but the other is roofless. We've pitched tents for the men for the present. That's why we wanted you ladies to bring along some supplies for Captain Hollander and his men."

Two piers stretched out into the water. Their boat headed for the one farthest from the fort. Camille was disappointed. She had hoped to see the inside of the fort.

A group of men stood on the pier waiting for them. Camille straightened her bonnet and smoothed her hair, now sticky from the saltwater spray and probably as limp as her dress and bonnet. Her sisters looked damp as well, but as pretty as when they had left this morning. She smiled, knowing that the sight of them would give these poor soldiers and prisoners a moment of pleasure.

"Welcome, ladies," said one of the men on the pier. "Major Warren asked that we meet you and escort you to a room where Captain Hollander will be brought. We hope your trip wasn't too uncomfortable."

"No, sir. It was rather pleasant for us." Mrs. Hollander answered for the group and immediately looked around from building to building trying to find the prisoner stockade. One rough structure looked like the next.

Recognizing her mother's disappointment and

frustration, Camille placed a hand on her shoulders. "It won't be long."

As soon as they stepped off the boat onto the pier, the heat of the island surrounded them. It was morning, but the glare of the white sand already hurt Camille's eyes as she carefully stepped along the plank path to the barracks. Her high-topped shoes prevented sand from getting into her stockings, but she could hear the gritting on the soles. A deep empathy for the men, both Union and Confederate, settled over her. Life here had to be difficult.

"This is where you're to remain until Captain Hollander is brought to you." Their escort opened a door to a newly constructed room, still smelling of fresh-cut pine. "We'll return these baskets to you once we've examined them."

Camille stood quietly next to her mother. No one said a word as they surveyed the room. Except for a small table and five crude chairs, the room was bare. Even the newly hewn wood couldn't take away the forlorn feeling that permeated every empty corner.

Within minutes, the door opened. Several guards deposited their baskets on the floor, then stepped aside to allow Charles to enter. "Captain Hollander, we've explained the rules to you. Two guards will be outside the door," said one of the soldiers as he unlocked a set of handcuffs on Charles.

Charles stood in the entrance squinting to see inside the dim room.

"Charles," Mrs. Hollander said quietly as she walked to him and slowly put her arms around his thin body.

"Mama," Charles whispered. He hugged his mother and buried his face in her hair.

The lump in Camille's throat threatened to suffocate her. She struggled to control her emotions even though her mother's quiet sobs broke the silence of the room.

Charles finally looked up and held his mother at arm's length. "You haven't changed a bit, Mama." He wiped a tear from under one of her eyes. He then looked toward the girls. "But I can't say the same for those three." He stepped away from his mother. "Aren't you going to give a brother a hug?"

Dorothy and Katherine ran and fell into his arms.

"This has to be Dorothy because she was the taller when I left, but I'm not real sure. These are two ladies, Mama."

"Oh, Charles, you're joshing with us," said Dorothy. He held them both and kissed them.

Camille stood back and let her sisters have their hugs, then he looked at her. "Camille, my goodness, is that you? Where's my little sister?"

Camille stepped into his embrace and melted against the soiled uniform coat. For a moment, she pushed aside the fact that they were in a prison camp and relished the feel of his arms around her. Her brother. Her strength.

He held her tight. She felt the catch of his breath in his throat. Heard his sniffle. Then with a shudder, he stepped away. "I can't believe it's really you. You're a lady. A full-grown lady."

"You've grown too, Charles. You don't look like a kid anymore. You look good."

"I guess we all change in two years, don't we?"

They sat around the table, reminiscing about the days before the war, then Charles told them about his two years. During the course of the day, Mrs. Hollander brought out bits of food that Charles attacked at first, then slowed down to enjoy. They listened in horror to the tales he had to tell, but mostly he wanted to know about home and how they had managed and who had returned from the war.

"So you've put on Dad's shoes, have you, Camille? I really hate what this war's done to my girls."

"Oh, no, don't ever say that," Mama said. "Nothing is worse than the death of our boys."

He swallowed another bite of pie. "I don't mean it in comparison to that. It just hurts me to think of what all of you are having to go through, and knowing that none of this was your fault." He rubbed his hand over Katherine's hair. "My sisters are beautiful. They shouldn't have to be doing what they're doing."

"Oh, for goodness' sake, Charles," interrupted Camille. "We're capable of bearing our burden as much as anyone. I think we've fared just fine, if you ask me."

"Speak for yourself," threw in Dorothy.

Camille had to laugh at her little sister. "No, Dorothy, I'm speaking for all of us. You know good and well we haven't had it bad compared to some of the stories I've heard about the families around Atlanta. We've been fortunate."

Mama got up and walked to a small window. "It looks so forlorn out here," she said. "How long will you be here?"

"I don't know. Sometimes officers are moved elsewhere. Sometimes they stay with their men. Since we're the first ones out on this island, who's to say what they'll do."

Charles walked over by his mother and placed his arms around her. "I'll be fine. Don't worry. I can't believe you're actually here though. I can't believe the major allowed this."

Camille answered her brother a little too quickly. "We were told it was because you're an officer."

Charles looked confused, but didn't answer.

Black menacing clouds darkened the sky south of the island. "As much as I would love to have y'all stay and visit longer," Charles said, "I think we need to get those men to take you back to the mainland before that weather reaches us. Those open boats aren't meant to take a storm."

Reluctantly, last hugs were given. Mama held on to her son as long as possible.

A hard knock at the door interrupted them. Sergeant Stafford stood outside the door out of breath. "I was on my way here when the guard met me. Major Warren ordered us to get you off the island immediately. So, please, ladies, get your things and hurry."

"Do as he says." Charles helped his mother fix the bonnet and gave her one last hug. "It's going to be okay, Mama. I'm safer here than on the battlefield, so think of that if you get sad."

The girls followed their escort out of the cabin, down the planked walkway, and onto the pier. Before getting into the boat, Camille watched Charles being led toward the stockade. A horrible sadness descended upon her, but when he looked her way, she smiled and waved to him one last time.

Everywhere she looked, soldiers, both white and black men in blue uniforms and Confederate prisoners, stared at them from behind wire fences. Camille's heart went out to all of them. Soldiers isolated on a desolate island. Men being caged like animals. The killing and the bloodshed on the battlefield weren't here, but the suffering was present nonetheless.

Sergeant Stafford touched her arm. "Miss Hollander, please. We need to hurry."

"I'm sorry. Of course."

Camille allowed herself to be helped into the boat. Once settled, she looked at the pier nearest the fort. There, talking with another man, was Major Warren, standing with his legs apart, looking as impressive as ever. Camille's breath caught. Trying not to be too obvious as the boat pulled away, she turned her head to look at him.

From across the distance of two piers their gazes locked. His eyes showed no emotion, no apology for staring, not even any friendliness or acknowledgment of recognition. It was just a stare, unnerving and bold.

She watched him until the boat turned, and when she looked back, he was gone.

Disappointment settled over her. She wasn't sure what she'd expected, but not having talked with the major left her feeling empty.

She'd heard that most of the Union officers were rude and arrogant. Major Jake Warren was probably no different. Still, his presence made her aware of herself as a woman as no other man had done before. She touched her warm face with her gloved hand and hoped no one could feel the heat that radiated from her agitated body.

A slight breeze touched her skin, cooling the nervous perspiration and lifting the sadness she felt from leaving Charles out here. She hoped Major Warren had a shred of decency in him where his prisoners were concerned. Having made the effort to get them out to the island gave her hope that he was capable of feeling compassion.

She looked beyond the fort. A wall of dark clouds rolled closer to the island, bringing with it a breeze that was a welcomed relief. She shuddered with the knowledge that a gentle breeze could turn into a monstrous wind within minutes, churning the sound waters into mountains of waves capable of sweeping under a boat their size.

She pulled her thin shawl tightly around her shoulders as the men positioned their oars in the locks. A group of men gathered at the end of the pier, and as if the distance between them and the boat made it okay to speak to the ladies, they all waved and yelled their good-byes.

Dorothy and Katherine returned their waves.

The three men at the oars maneuvered the little boat expertly into the open water. To Camille there appeared nothing in the distance, and she wondered how they could find their way to the coastline. She knew that eventually if they went north they'd end up on the mainland, but it amazed her how they would keep their course.

Early in the war, the light had been removed from the lighthouse on shore to prevent Union ships from finding the channel, though it had not prevented the ones determined to get into the Biloxi area. She hoped her three men could do the same today and do it quickly before the squall reached them.

The Hollander women settled against one another without saying a word. Camille knew her mother's thoughts were on Charles, and she let her relish her memories of the few hours she'd had with him. Dorothy and Katherine leaned against each other and closed their eyes.

It wasn't long before the waves coming in from the west began to knock against the boat. The three men struggled to keep the boat on course. Their knuckles strained white and beads of sweat popped out on their brows. The relentless waves pushed the boat more and more to the east.

Camille held onto the seat tightly and tried to think of something to do to help, but nothing came to mind. A feeling of helplessness engulfed her. Spray from the waves battered everyone. The lightweight bonnet quickly became saturated and dripped water into her eyes. Her wet shawl stuck to her body and produced no warmth from the sudden drop in temperature. She shivered and wrapped her arm around her mother's shoulders and pulled her to her body.

Sergeant Stafford leaned forward and said something to Private Martin and yelled something to Sergeant Allen, who nodded.

Sergeant Stafford turned. "Ladies, we're going to have to return to the island. There's no way we'll be able to keep our course with these waves and the direction of the wind. If that weather hits harder while we're in the middle out here, we might as well throw our oars overboard, and it's coming up faster than we thought." He shouted over the crash of the waves against the sides of the boat.

"Do you think it's safe to row into it?" asked Mrs. Hollander.

"I think we have a better chance to get back there

than to make it for the nine miles or so we have left. The waves will at least be at our backs." He grimaced as he strained against his oars.

On command the three men worked their oars until the boat turned, producing a torrent of spray as one wave after another hit the boat from different directions at once. Finally, the waves came at them only from the stern, shooting the boat quickly to shore.

Katherine and Dorothy looked horrified. Camille couldn't remember the last time the girls had been in a boat except to travel the calm waters of the bay back and forth to Biloxi.

"Girls, it's okay," she shouted over the wind. "These men know what they're doing."

Camille had her doubts. The island didn't seem to be any closer. She hoped she wasn't good at judging distances.

Time dragged. The waves crested higher and higher. Spray from the water beaded on everyone and rolled down as if from perspiration.

Sergeant Stafford turned around and faced Camille. "Are you okay, Miss Hollander?"

"We're fine. I'm sure you'll get us back to the island safely."

He forced a nod, but he had not reassured her in the least bit. In fact, Camille felt as if her life had been placed in the hands of a young boy, and even though he was doing the best he could, she was afraid it wouldn't be enough. She couldn't be angry with him, but she could certainly be angry with that major. He should have assigned an older, more experienced man to transport them back or waited for the storm to pass.

Camille strained with the men as they fought the oars. Her body ached from the tension and the dampness. She squeezed her eyes shut. Silently she prayed for their safety.

When she opened her eyes she caught her first glimpse of the sand beach. The waves had pushed them past the end of the island where they had started, but land in any shape or form would be better than being caught in the open water in a small boat.

Within minutes, the men jumped into the turbulent water and tugged the boat by hand toward the beach. They made progress until they reached a step-up right by the water's edge. With each step upward, the waves pushed at least one of the men backward and all of them went with him.

Camille sat stunned and helpless as she watched the men struggle in a seemingly hopeless attempt to beach the boat. Water rushed against and around their bodies with a force that lifted them off the bottom while the boat tossed dangerously close behind them.

The women gripped the sides of the boat, but kept their anxieties to themselves until a huge wave crashed against Private Martin, taking him under. Dorothy screamed and threw herself against Katherine. After several long, agonizing minutes, the private appeared hanging onto a rope.

Together the three men struggled with the boat until a blessed wave lifted them at the right moment over the step-up and the boat touched the sand.

Sergeant Stafford held the side of the boat. "Ladies, hurry. Jump before she turns over."

Camille popped up from her seat, hiked her skirt up around her thighs, and jumped over the sides. Water immediately rushed around her, spinning her until one of the men grabbed her from behind. Getting her balance, she turned to help the others. When her mother jumped, Camille took her arm and helped the sergeant lead her to higher ground. One of the other men helped her sisters while the third struggled with the boat. As soon as the men buried the anchor in the sand, fierce gusts of wind hit from the west, pounding them with horizontal bullets of rain.

Camille looked upward and gave thanks for making it to shore. A tremor of fear worked its way down her body as she shifted her gaze out to the turbulent waters, now violently whipping waves higher than their boat.

The four Hollander women, standing on a narrow strip of sand, huddled together for strength as they faced yet another storm.

Chapter Five

Major Jake Warren knew he'd made a mistake. He cursed under his breath for sending the women back to the mainland in what was turning out to be dangerous weather. Shouting orders to tie everything down for an afternoon of storms, he ran up the circular stairs of the fort.

Standing next to the guard on lookout duty, Jake raised his telescope. Gray water and white caps clouded his vision.

"Blasted women," he said out loud. When the guard looked at him curiously, he turned away. Even as he'd given the orders to have the Hollander women brought out to the island, he knew there would be trouble. The more he thought about it, the madder he got, not at the women, but at himself.

He knew why he had sent for them. Other prisoners had families close by, but he hadn't bothered to contact them. It was imperative, though, for him to send for the captain's family. He hadn't admitted it to himself then, but he knew the reason for his haste. Many nights he had tossed and turned thinking about Camille, and he knew he had to see her again.

Once they'd made it to the island, he forced himself to stay in the background, but he knew every move Camille and her family made.

Every man on the island knew of the women's arrival, and one way or another they all stood where they too could see them. He wondered if anyone else saw in Camille what he did, or if he had imagined her allure. As the ladies walked down the pier, he watched the men around him. They followed the women with their eyes, and he knew that they were drawn to the one in the mint green dress as he had been.

"Major, I think I have the boat in sight," the guard shouted over the wind.

Jake turned his glass to the east and found the tiny speck on the water, but it wasn't heading to the fort.

"I think it's going to land about a mile or so down the beach," the guard said.

Cursing inwardly, Jake stared into the glass. "I was afraid this wind would keep them from getting back here. It's right out of the northwest. Not good."

He took the steps of the stair tower two at a time and shouted for horses to be saddled, then he headed to his room to grab rain gear. It had only begun to sprinkle, but he knew what was in store.

Jake waited impatiently outside the fort for the rest of his men. The wind whipped around the curved structure, stinging him with bits of sand. Below him the waves crashed against the pier, reminding him that somewhere along the shoreline Camille and her family were possibly fighting for their lives.

He stepped a few feet from the wall of the fort and shouted up to the lookout. "Can you still see their boat?"

"No, sir, I think it must've beached somewhere on the other side of the bend."

Four soldiers in rain slicks came out of the fort. Without further ado, he led them to the stables and mounted his big black stallion, Moses.

The group zigzagged their way through the buildings. As they passed the prisoner stockade, he wondered what he'd do with the prisoners if the weather turned into a full-fledged storm. The one completed shelter couldn't hold all of them. It was a problem he hoped he wouldn't have to face. Right now his only concern was getting to Camille.

The group made good time riding along the gently curved north beach until they reached the bend where a structure was being built to house a lighthouse. Several men, crouched down against the structure under rain slicks, saluted Jake. He returned the salute.

The soldiers watched as the major's group rode

past the lighthouse, probably wondering what they were doing. Not many people ventured past this area and certainly not in this weather.

Jake guided Moses down a narrow stretch of sand. The high water had covered much of the beach, making it difficult to find hard ground. The waves prevented them from using the water's edge, and high piles of seaweed, washed-up logs, and other debris made it impossible to get any farther inland.

"Come on, boy, you can do it." Moses picked up his legs briskly, neighed, and led the others.

Rain pelted the group, making it hard to see more than a few feet in front of them. He strained to catch a glimpse of something, anything, to tell him the group was safe. He knew eventually he'd run into them by heading east, but it was impossible to drag his eyes away from the shoreline hoping to see them walking toward him.

Moses stumbled, caught himself immediately, then continued on his trek. "That'a boy. You did great."

He patted the horse's neck. He had complete confidence in his steed, but looking behind him, he knew the others would have a difficult time following in his path. Wind and rain burned his face as he watched several of his men dismount. They had to lead their horses, along with the spares, through the narrow strip of sloping beach he'd just maneuvered.

Impatience twisted his insides. Even Moses pulled

at his reins, needing to bolt down the beach as if he understood Jake's need.

Time dragged. The slow progress agitated him. It was all he could do not to leave the others and search on his own.

Directly in front of him lay a beached log, the size of half of a tree. Lying partially in the water, it swung around unpredictably with the crash of each wave. To avoid it, he turned Moses up into the steep slope of the inland grass.

From his vantage point at the top of the ridge, he scanned the shoreline through the heavy sheets of pounding rain that blurred his vision. He wiped his eyes and watched a tiny black figure in the distance. Pulling the reins, he strained to see movement. Then, as he watched, several more black spots appeared.

"I've spotted them," he shouted over the sound of the wind and waves.

His eyes stung as he pushed Moses ahead of his group. The big horse lunged into a slow gallop. Jake marveled at his ability to keep his footing in the sand. Within minutes, the black spots materialized into shapes of people.

"Right here, Major," Sergeant Stafford yelled as he waved his hands over his head. "Right here!"

Jake kneed Moses. For the first time in the last several hours, Jake breathed easier. Not knowing if the boat had made it to shore had eaten away at his heart. His insides ached to think what could have happened to Camille and her family. They were his responsibility, and seeing the rain-soaked group coming toward him lifted the weight from his shoulders and lightened his heart.

He counted. Everyone was there.

He jumped off his horse when he reached them.

"Sir, we tried to make it. We couldn't." Sergeant Stafford, holding up Mrs. Hollander, was breathless, soaked, and pale.

"I know, Sergeant. I'm just glad you're all safe."

Jake looked from the young man to Mrs. Hollander. Her eyes met his for a second, then she turned away. Jake couldn't blame her. He had put her family at risk.

Camille looked up at Jake. "Thank you for coming for us." Her bonnet hung in her face. Her hair was matted and straggly, but her smile warmed his heart. She was gorgeous.

"Are you all right?"

"I think so," she said, "but I had my doubts there for a while."

Her smile wrenched his heart because it couldn't hide the fear in her eyes. For someone who had lived around water all of her life and who stood up to a troop of soldiers, she looked terrified. He fought the urge to pull her into his arms and hold her until her fears subsided. But that wasn't possible. Others stood around them, not to mention the fact that she'd probably bolt from him if he tried to comfort her.

In his dreams, Camille Hollander might have warm feelings for him, but in reality, he was the enemy who confiscated her salt and was now holding her brother captive. It would have to be a dream for her to see him for anything other than that.

"I'm glad all of you are okay," he finally said.

The sound of the other riders approaching gave him reason to look away, relieved.

Jake instructed Sergeant Stafford's men to get on the spare horses. Martin and Allen offered to take Dorothy and Katherine on their horses. Jake pointed to one of the other men to assist Mrs. Hollander. Then he looked at Camille. "You ride with me."

Before Camille could answer, Jake had mounted the big animal again, moved alongside of her, and hoisted her effortlessly onto the horse's back and clamped her against him with an arm around her waist.

"Everyone try to stay together," he shouted, then turned the horse to head back toward the fort.

Camille grabbed the saddle horn and dared not look at the ground far below or to think about the body that held her close. She wasn't sure what was worse, falling onto the sand and being trampled by the animal or leaning up against the man who had invaded her dreams for weeks.

Shifting in the saddle, she wrestled with the wet skirt that stuck to her thighs and bunched up underneath her body. She moved to try to make herself more comfortable. Jake's right arm circled her waist. He loosened his grip to allow her to shift around.

The small saddle jammed her back and thighs into his body. Her faced burned knowing she rubbed against him with each movement. Finally, she quit moving and hoped he wasn't aware of how close she fit against him. With the rain beating against her face, she closed her eyes and prayed that she could endure the glorious torture.

Unexpectedly, he moved his arm from around her, leaving her cold and vulnerable, but she didn't ask what he was about to do.

"Let me put this around you," he whispered low and hoarse into her ear. "I think we can both fit under it." He had unfastened his rain cape and wrapped it around her body. She took the edges and pulled it close.

"This might be a little awkward, but it'll keep you drier."

She nodded her thank-you, but dared not turn.

Holding the reins with his left hand, he slipped his right one under the cape and rested it snugly on Camille's stomach. She stiffened.

"If you'll relax and lean against me, the ride won't be so hard on you," he said in her ear.

She tried, but it was difficult. Nothing stood between them but a thin layer of wet clothing. With each breath his chest heaved against her back, and with each demand he gave to his horse, the muscles in his legs tightened around her thighs.

He leaned close to her head. "Millie, if you don't relax, neither of us will make it back. I'm not going to hurt you."

The pet name that he'd used surprised her but it sent familiar warmth throughout her body. "I know that, sir. It's just hard for me to touch a strange man."

"A strange man?" he asked. "I'm hurt that you think I'm still a stranger."

The wind and rain howled around them and Jake had to put his mouth next to her ear for her to hear. With each word, Camille's body trembled. She couldn't get words out to respond to his last statement.

"You're freezing," he said and pulled her closer to him. "Now, try to relax. It's a long ride back to the fort."

Her taut muscles loosened, and gradually she let herself relax. When his arm tightened around her, she didn't protest. She snuggled against his big chest feeling secure and safer than she had in many years.

She smelled his masculinity, his muskiness. So unfamiliar, yet so soothing. Gradually, she moved more easily with the rhythm of the horse.

"That's better, isn't it?" he whispered close to her ear. "Enjoy the ride. After what you and your family have gone through today, you deserve to be comforted. And since I've mentioned it, I am sorry, Camille. Had I known that the weather would come up so fast, I wouldn't have dared to send you out in it."

She heard him swallow.

"You gave me a scare."

Turning her head, she finally faced him. With his lips just inches from her face, she felt his warm breath on her skin. This time it was her turn to swallow hard.

"We were all scared," she managed to say. "I felt sorry for the men. They felt responsible for us, but there wasn't much they could do once the wind picked up."

"No, it was my responsibility. I never would've forgiven myself had something happened to you." Then in an abrupt change of words, he added, "To you and your family."

But Camille had caught his first statement. He had said "you."

She twisted so that her gaze met his. "Thank you," she said softly.

For a long moment, with his lips just inches from hers, she thought they would touch. She wanted nothing more at the moment than for him to kiss her, to feel his mouth on hers, but the horse jerked. The spell was broken.

Jake looked away. He quickly yanked the reins to direct Moses more toward the water's edge before looking back at her with a quick smile.

She smiled back and put her head against his shoulder. Content to feel his body surrounding her, she relaxed and swayed with the movement of the horse. Gradually she eased into a light sleep.

Suddenly the horse stretched under her. Camille stiffened and sat up.

"Don't worry," he said as he maneuvered the horse up a steep incline. "We had to get off the beach for a moment. I hope the others can make it." He turned, taking his warmth with him.

She looked back at the others as they struggled up the slope. With the light dimming and the rain still beating down on them, she could hardly make out the faces of those behind her.

She shivered. He pulled her closer.

Neither spoke as they neared the western tip of the island. Too soon, Camille saw the lights from the buildings in the distance. Daylight had turned to darkness quickly. Rain still came down in sheets, and the wind still whipped around them, but Camille didn't want the ride to end. Being near Major Warren had awakened something in her that she had never experienced before. She sighed.

"Are you still cold?" he asked.

She shook her head. "No, Major."

"I'd appreciate it if you'd call me Jake when we're alone."

She shifted to face him and was met by a devastating smile.

"Jake." His name slid across her tongue easily before vanishing into the wind. She opened her lips to form the name again, but as she looked into his eyes, she was unable to move. Could hardly breathe.

He lowered his head and touched his lips to hers. She closed her eyes. She didn't pull away. Except for a few friendly pecks from suitors before the war, no one had ever kissed her before, not like this. She wanted it to last forever.

But it was Jake who pulled away. Slowly he ran his lips along the contours of her cheek, kissed her closed eyelids, then placed his face against her hair.

Camille never wanted the moment to end, but remembering her family behind her, she turned. The little group had gotten closer, but in the dark she knew they had not witnessed the most incredible moment of her life.

Relieved, she settled against his chest again.

"Just relax. We're almost to the fort."

She didn't want to be home, or at the fort, or anywhere but here in his arms, but she nodded.

Without more words between them, their bodies moved together in rhythm with Moses as they made their way around the last curve of the island.

"That's where you started," he said as he interrupted her dreams.

"That didn't take long," she said.

"Long enough," he answered and smiled a crooked sort of smile.

Soldiers ran out of buildings to meet the group. Jake became Major Warren once again. He snapped out orders in answer to the many questions thrown at him.

"Sergeant, take the women to my quarters. There'll be sufficient dry bedding for all of them there. Tell the other men in the room to take the necessities to sleep elsewhere tonight. Have some warm food sent to them."

"Yes, sir," he answered.

Jake turned Moses and addressed Mrs. Hollander. "Follow the sergeant and make sure all of you stay in the room. You'll be warm and safe in the fort. Use whatever clothing is available. There are six other officers who share the room, but they won't mind if you use any of the clothing. My personal belongings are at the far end of the room. Use what you need." At that he lifted Camille off the horse and with a kick of the stirrup he was gone.

Camille found herself in the midst of strange men again. She ran toward her mother and helped her off the horse. Together they were led through the sally port then into the bowels of the fort. Even in the darkness and confusion of the storm, she could feel the impressiveness of the bricked structure.

Her mother tripped. Grabbing her by the shoulders, Camille pulled her close. Tired and haggard, Mrs. Hollander leaned limply against Camille. Camille had never seen her mother in such condition. She, like Camille, had helped everyone else in the village, finding strength and hope when others lost theirs. Now, her mother's helplessness frightened her.

Her sisters, each being helped by the same young men as before, were doing just fine. Katherine's face was animated. She smiled in spite of the mass of windblown, wet hair that fell from under her bonnet. Dorothy's sad face couldn't conceal the sparkle in her eyes as a young soldier worried over her. Camille knew she wouldn't have to worry about them.

Sergeant Stafford approached them from the rear and reached out for Mrs. Hollander. "Let me help you, Miss Camille."

"Thank you, Sergeant, but I'm afraid you need as much help as I do."

Mrs. Hollander surprised Camille. "Let him help. He's been a perfect gentleman throughout all of this hideous episode."

"Yes, ma'am, I know he has." Camille let the sergeant help her mother, but inwardly she fumed. Her mother hadn't said it, but Camille knew what she'd implied. Stafford had been a gentleman in comparison to others, and Camille knew who the other one was. She was afraid that the major had quickly lost his gentleman status in her mother's eyes by sending them into the storm.

She was about to say something in defense of Major Warren, but they arrived at the room. Hesitating at the door for a second, she let her eyes become adjusted to the dim light inside where several lanterns burned on small bedside tables. Tall shadows danced along the towering walls, making the room strangely foreboding, but the dryness and warmth struck her right away and willingly she stepped inside.

"We'll leave you ladies alone. Major Warren said

to dry off and to get in bed to warm up. We'll have food sent in as soon as we can get some together. Things are a bit chaotic right now with this weather. We're still trying to get some of our prisoners out of the weather. I beg your patience."

"Thank you, sir. We appreciate your help," Mrs. Hollander spoke up again. "We can manage now. You go take care of the prisoners. Take care of my son."

It didn't take the girls long to strip off their wet clothes and to don pieced-together outfits. After hanging their dresses up to dry, each crawled into a cot.

Camille took the far corner of the room, where, behind a partition, lay the private world of the major.

She crawled between clean sheets that smelled of sunshine. She was impressed. Pulling the rough covers up to her chin, she let her gaze roam across the tiny area. It wasn't what she'd expected. She counted fifteen books stacked neatly against one of the wall, and she wondered how he had accumulated so many. His clothes were neatly folded and placed on top of a large black chest. Several dress shirts and a dress uniform hung along one wall.

Major Jake Warren was a mystery to her. Now that she was aware of his gentler side, it was hard for her to remember the revulsion she had felt toward him on their first meeting. She ached to know more about the man who protected her and soothed her fears that afternoon.

He was a Yankee officer, her enemy, but there was something more to him that fascinated her.

The shadows from the kerosene lanterns flickered against the walls as she let her mind float through disjointed images of the man until she was incapable of fighting off sleep.

Thunder exploded in the darkness. Through the fog of sleep, Camille felt the waves crashing against the side of the boat and wind whipping across her face.

Lightning popped. She sat up straight in her cot and pulled the cover up to her chin. She gasped for air as the muscles throughout her body tightened. Horrified, she was unable to move.

Then her mind cleared. The next bolt of lightning lit the sky through the iron shutters outside the window of the room. The tension flowed from her body as she remembered that she was in Jake's room. Jake's bed.

She swung her legs over the side of the cot and sat up. The enormous pair of pants and shirt she'd borrowed hung on her. She pulled them closer to her body, then tiptoed to peek around the partition. Her mother and sisters slept soundly.

She wanted to venture out into the fort to find Jake, but remembering his warning to stay in the room, she returned to her bed and pulled the covers up once again. The small slits in the shutter could not keep out the light from one streak of lightning after another. A real storm had developed and she wondered where Jake was. Was he safe? Was Charles one of the prisoners out in the elements?

Thunder crashed and lightning exploded somewhere close by. She closed her eyes and cringed.

When she opened them again, she saw a silhouette at the entrance of the partition.

"Jake, is that you?"

Jake took a step toward the bed. "I didn't want to wake you. I was checking to make sure all of you got settled."

He walked over to the cot and knelt down. He was inches from her.

"We've had some problems," he said, "and I haven't been able to get in here. Have you eaten?"

"No, I think I must have fallen asleep before the men brought the food in. I'm not hungry though."

"Are you sure?" he asked. "I can find something for you."

"No, no. You get back to your men. I'm just fine."

Jake kneeled over her. Camille couldn't see the features in his face, but she sensed him looking at her. Neither said anything. Finally, he leaned down and kissed her on the lips, very gently, very softly.

He stood up. "I have to get back."

Her heart pounded against her chest. "Where will you sleep?"

"No one is actually sleeping. The weather is much too threatening for anyone to rest. I'm fine. Don't worry."

"Jake," she asked with hesitation, "what about the prisoners?"

"They're all right. We moved the lot of them without permanent structures around so that everyone is out of the rain. They're crowded, but safe."

"Thank you," she whispered.

"Charles is fine, Camille. I can't show partiality, but he's an officer and will be treated accordingly."

Again the silence between them was unbearable.

"Uh, do you mind if I change into a dry shirt? This one is soaked."

He didn't wait for her to answer, but reached into a stack of folded laundry and pulled out something to wear. Camille swallowed hard when he stripped away the rain slick and shirt from his back. Grabbing a towel, he dried his face and hair and then his chest. The light was dim, but she caught every movement he made.

Never before had she been with a man in so personal a situation. She knew she shouldn't watch him, but nothing could make her look away.

During rounds nursing the soldiers, she had seen men in all states of dress and undress, but she saw them only as patients.

This was different. This man had kissed her on the lips and held her close to him as they made their way back to the fort.

Heavens, just thinking about it made her breath hitch.

Finally, he leaned back down to her. "Do you need anything?"

She found her voice. "No, we're okay now that we're dry and in here. You need to take care of yourself, though, so you won't catch pneumonia."

She felt him kneel against the bed. "Please don't worry." He reached out and smoothed her hair away from her face. "You stay here so you don't get sick."

He slowly lowered his face to her, but instead of kissing her on the mouth as she wanted, he kissed her in an almost fatherly manner on the forehead.

"Sweet dreams," he said and left.

The wind howled around the fort, but Camille heard it only vaguely. Jake's presence filled her senses even after he left the room. Again and again she relived the touch of his hand on her face and the touch of his lips to hers.

She wanted to talk with him again, to be with him, but she knew it was impossible. How could she see him in the morning without showing her emotions? Tomorrow, how would she tell him good-bye?

Sunlight sneaked through the cracks in the shutters. The difference in the air told her that the storm was over.

"Well, did you finally wake up?" teased Dorothy as

Camille walked up to the group outside in the court-yard.

She ignored her sister's jab. "Yes, I did sleep late this morning, didn't I? She tore off a piece of hot bread handed to her by a soft-spoken black man. "Thank you, this smells delicious. Did you bake it?"

"Yessum, I did. My name's Lucius. I cook for the major and the men in the fort. It's not often we get nice ladies like you here so I hope the bread is special." He spoke, but avoided Camille's eyes.

Camille took a big bite. "Umm, it's great. It tastes as good as it smells."

She listened to her sisters jabber about the horrible boat ride and storm. She responded appropriately, but as she talked, she searched the interior of the fort for signs of Jake. She hoped to get a few minutes alone with him before the boat left, but she was afraid it wouldn't happen.

"Excuse me, ladies," said a young officer as he walked up to them. "Major Warren gave permission for you to see Captain Hollander before you leave, but you'll need to follow me now. Your boat will be leaving shortly."

Camille searched the premises of the fort as she followed her sisters and mother, but Jake was nowhere to be seen. As they entered one of the outbuildings, Charles greeted them with a flurry of curses and threats aimed at Major Warren and the Union Army in general. He ranted and raved about the danger his family had been placed in, then fussed about the crowded accommodations given to the prisoners.

Nothing they said could calm him down so Camille finally sat with her frightened sisters and mother and let him vent.

When the visit was over, Camille breathed a sigh of relief. Her heart went out to her brother, but she was more concerned that his anger would create problems for him. She wished she could talk with Jake once more to get reassurance that Charles would be safe.

Two unfamiliar soldiers escorted them quickly to a boat. Disappointment settled around Camille for not having seen Jake, but she was sure he was busy with the storm's aftermath.

Waiting for her turn to be helped into the boat, Camille's arm was grabbed from behind.

Jake stood inches from her with tired eyes and a heavy shadow of a beard. "I'm sorry I couldn't come see you this morning. I've been busy. I hope you've been treated well."

Camille's heart pounded, but she spoke with a calm voice. "Yes, thank you for asking. We've been fine." She wanted to say more, but her mother was already in the boat watching them, a scowl creasing her brow.

"It's obvious your mother isn't pleased with our

hospitality," Jake said in a low voice. "I hope she won't hold it against me."

"Mama had a terrible scare yesterday. She's very worried about Charles. We saw him this morning, and, I have to admit, it wasn't pleasant. He was upset and I'm sure it upset her."

"I'm sorry about everything, but your mother has to understand this is a prisoner-of-war camp and her son is a prisoner. He's an officer in the Confederate Army, our enemy. He's our prisoner."

"We're aware of that, Major Warren, but she's still his mother, and it hurts to see him and the other men in these conditions."

Jake's eyes turned gray. "These conditions are a lot better than most of the camps he could've been sent to. You can thank God he didn't end up in Andersonville."

Just the name of the camp sent a shiver down Camille's spine. "We know that, but you still have to understand our position," Camille said, choosing her words carefully.

"Your position is obvious to all of us. You're loyal to the Confederacy. We're not."

His words cut into Camille's heart. What he said was true, but it wasn't what she wanted to hear.

He continued, "I was hoping to see you again under better circumstances, but I guess there'll be no better conditions."

Camille wasn't sure what he meant, but there was

no time to further the discussion. Jake began giving orders to the men in the boat. One of the men reached out to help her into the boat. She wanted Jake to ask them to stay longer, but it didn't happen.

Jake turned to Mrs. Hollander. "I do apologize for the inconvenience you've been caused. If you'll trust us again, I'll see to it you visit your son again."

"Thank you, Major Warren. I'll accept your apology only because I do want to see my son again."

"Mother," Camille said a little too loudly, "the major has been kind enough to let us visit Charles, and I would think you'd appreciate what he did."

"That will be enough out of you, Camille Rene. Of course I appreciate it, and the major knows it," she said curtly.

Camille looked at Jake with pleading eyes, but his look told her that pleading would do no good. He had been insulted for his act of kindness, and he wouldn't forget it.

"I hope your trip will be more pleasant than yesterday's. I'm certain it will be. The water is almost slick calm today. Sergeant, cast off and be careful." He tipped his hat. "Ladies, have a nice day."

Camille smoldered. Her mother had been rude. Jake Warren hadn't been much better. Why hadn't he tried to console her mother? She dared to look back up toward the pier one more time. Jake walked quickly in the opposite direction as if a burden had been unloaded.

Again Camille fumed. She hadn't imagined their two kisses. Why did he act as if nothing had happened?

She stared into the crystal blue-green water.

Men were a mystery to her, and after today, she was sure, they'd stay that way for quite some time.

Chapter Six

Major Warren put on an extra shirt. The chill inside the fort indicated the harshness of the November weather outside. The winds on the western end of the island were biting as they swept across the level island sands. Just a few months ago, the soldiers were complaining of the tortuous heat. Now they shivered with the cold and humidity.

The prisoner situation tugged at his heart. Yes, they were the enemy, but they were human and having over one thousand of them on the island made it impossible to provide adequate shelter.

Each day he secretly checked on Captain Hollander. He had told Mrs. Hollander the family could visit with him again, but he kept putting the visit off. Now the wintry weather prevented an open boat trip for the women.

Had the women come, Camille would have been with them, and he couldn't let himself see her again. For long lonely nights he had lain awake thinking of the girl. Her memory tugged at his insides as no girl had ever done. She haunted him no matter how much he tried to forget.

He wasn't sure how old the girl was, but he guessed that she couldn't be more than in her early twenties. He was thirty-four, but even more than the age difference, he was a Union officer. The age, the differences in their culture, and this war made his thinking about the girl hopeless. Getting her out of his system was imperative.

But how? He still felt the softness of her lips. He shouldn't have kissed her, either on the horse or in the fort, but he had no control. Now he regretted it.

Taking his coat down from the hanger, he pulled it tightly against his chest. For the past couple of days he had been coughing from chest congestion. Pneumonia was a killer here. He had to be careful. The camp surgeon had been called into New Orleans recently to help out at the hospital there, so no one was on the island to help him or the prisoners if the need arose.

Not that the surgeon could do any good. The best he could do was to saw off legs and ration out the little medicine that got as far as the island.

Jake helped himself to a piece of warm bread and a cup of strong coffee as he passed the courtyard oven. Neither he nor Lucius spoke beyond the necessary good-mornings because of the biting cold. He then greeted two guards huddled together for warmth as he passed through the salle port and onto the wharf.

He pulled his coat tighter to his body, then walked across the wooden walkway out toward the stockades. The general bakery situated midway between the fort and the stockade appeared to be on fire with so much steam coming up from its windows and smokestacks. The aroma permeated the entire complex. The food from this bakery was not as good as Lucius', but for a prisoner of war camp, it wasn't bad. He stuck his head inside, checked on the prisoners who worked there, then made his way around the remaining sites of his rounds.

Getting back inside the fort almost an hour later was a relief. Without the constant wind, the cold didn't seem quite so bad. He tossed his coat on a bench. He had two more spots to check before filling out his paperwork, and those included the two cells that the soldiers dubbed "the dungeon." They held the troublemakers, the prisoners who caused problems even for the other prisoners.

Right now the men he'd captured in the bayou occupied those cells and awaited their transfer to New Orleans. Captain Avery, as he was called, and his band of marauders had wreaked havoc with the local citizens and with solitary boats from his fort. They were deserters who lived off those trying to bring the war to a close.

Since Jake had captured them, the burden of housing them lay on his shoulders. Just as soon as the orders arrived, he'd be able to ship them off to New Orleans to be dealt with by the courts, but until then he'd have to deal with their problems.

Jake met one of the guards as he entered the dark circular halls leading to the cells.

"Sir, I was just coming to get you."

"What's wrong, Sergeant?"

"Avery and his men aren't acting normal."

Jake laughed before the man could finish. "What's normal for that crew?"

"Yes, sir, I agree," said the young guard, "but they're banding together, humming, singing, laughing loud, doing anything to make the guards upset. We just think they're up to something."

It was the last thing Jake wanted to hear, but it was his job to keep problems from flaring. "I'm on my way there now, so I'll check it out."

Jake followed the young man to the entrance of the cells where a guard opened the first barred door with a large key. The two men followed Jake down into a dark passageway where Jake opened the second barred door, lifted a handgun out of his holster, and stepped inside.

No laughing or singing was going on. As his eyes

adjusted to the dim light, he counted five men against the far corner of the room.

"Where's Avery?" he demanded.

"Right here, Major," but before Jake could turn, Avery jumped from a dark corner of the room, knocked the gun from Jake's hand, and slammed him against the cold wall. He looked straight into Avery's eyes, but could say nothing. A fire that started in his right shoulder consumed his entire body and almost paralyzed his movements. As if in slow motion, Jake watched Avery's sickening grin spread across his face. Looking down, Jake saw the handle of a knife sticking out of his shoulder.

He wanted to reach down to pull out the knife, but his arms refused to cooperate. Avery took care of the knife. With one quick motion, he yanked the knife out of his flesh, leaving Jake on the verge of unconsciousness.

Avery spun him around and imprisoned him with his arms. Jake was at his mercy. He fought to stay conscious. He knew Avery was holding him up against his body and forcing him out in front of him, but there was nothing he could do to stop it. Closing his eyes, he fought the excruciating pain. He needed to scream, but even that didn't come.

When he opened his eyes again, he was outside the fort being pushed toward the end of the wharf. He hadn't remembered getting here, but he knew he couldn't pass out again.

One of the larger gunboats lay at the end of the pier. Avery shoved him toward it, but even in his half-conscious state, Jake knew that if he got into the boat, he had no chance of survival.

As Avery's hold momentarily loosened to get into the boat, Jake took a deep breath and threw himself in the opposite direction. His body lunged over the side of the pier.

Gunshots exploded instantly above him as he sank into the silence of the freezing water.

With his eyes shut tight, he sank into the deep water. Numbness from the frigid cold eased his pain. He floated in blackness, not fighting the weightlessness. He held on to consciousness by a whisper.

His body touched the hard sand of the bottom, bringing him back to his senses. This was not the way he wanted to die. Struggling to keep his lungs from inhaling the strangling water, he pushed himself upward where he grabbed a piling with his right hand. The sharp edges of the barnacles sliced into his hand, but he refused to let go. His life depended on his staying above the water.

He watched as the boat on the other side of the pier pulled away. Gunshots still popped from all directions, and Jake wondered how many of Avery's men made it out.

He closed his eyes again as hot pain shot across his body.

* * *

Because of the November chill in the air, Camille stayed in bed later than normal. Food supplies were extremely low. No matter how cold it was, she had to fish that morning. The midmorning sun shone weakly through a ceiling of low clouds as she finally headed off into the channel.

Several small boats passed her by. Hellos were exchanged with the other fishermen trying to feed their families as she was doing. From the corner of her eye she watched another boat coming in from the sound and wondered, hoped even, that it was one from the island. There hadn't been any news of Charles for months.

In her mind she even envisioned Jake being in the boat, but when it got closer, she realized that it was Sergeant Stafford.

She pulled the oars up and waited until their boats got closer. "Hello, Sergeant."

Sergeant Stafford turned her way and waved cautiously, but Camille could tell that he didn't recognize her.

"It's me, Camille," she shouted.

He opened his eyes with recognition. "I'm so sorry," he said, "but with that god-awful hat you're wearing, it's hard to know who you are." His boat pulled up alongside of hers. "You're just the person we came to see. Can you come to shore? I need to talk with you."

"Certainly." Her stomach muscles contracted. Why

was he here? Had something happened to Charles? Had something happened to Jake?

All sorts of wild ideas flowed through her mind as she made her way to the pier.

"Please, have the men come inside where it's warm. We can talk in there. Mama is down the road, but my sisters are inside cooking."

She led them into the house, took off her hat, allowing her mane of black hair to cascade down her back, not unnoticed by the men who silently took their places around the fireplace. When she turned, they were all watching her.

"What's the matter?" she asked pointedly. "I get the feeling that this isn't a social call. Is something wrong?"

The men looked at one another. "Something is wrong and we need your help. We captured one of the bayou marauders. He got hold of a knife two days ago. He and his bunch escaped. They stabbed the major."

Camille paled and braced herself against the wall.

Sergeant Stafford jumped up and placed his hand on her arm for support. "I'm sorry. I didn't mean to alarm you."

Camille steadied herself. "I'm fine. What about Jake, uh, Major Warren?"

"Major Warren needs some medical attention. The wound itself wasn't that serious because it was in the shoulder, but the knife was old and dirty and pretty rusty. I guess because of that Major Warren has come down with a terrible fever. Our camp surgeon is in New Orleans, and the other men who work in the hospital have done all they know how to do. I heard the major tell someone how you and your mother took care of the wounded around here. Do you think there's anything you could do for him?"

Camille's mind was already racing through the small inventory of medical supplies she and her mother had hoarded. "I can try. Give me a minute to get a few things together."

"Do you have pants or something warmer to wear than that thin dress?" the sergeant said.

Camille nodded and left the room with Dorothy in tow. "Millie, you can't just go to the island alone with those men. You have to wait for Mama to get back."

Camille kept moving. "I'll be fine, Dorothy. Mama will just have to understand."

"She won't. I can assure you she won't, especially if you go out there in pants."

As soon as she got into her room, Camille pulled off the fishing dress and reached for the trousers she'd worn on the road to New Orleans. "Dorothy, I know you're worried, but I'll be okay."

"That man's a Union soldier. He's holding our brother in his prison out there. There's no reason to risk your life for him. How can you possibly think about going?" Dorothy's voice was shrill and demanding.

Camille looked at her. How could she explain? Her sister could never understand the way she felt at the moment. She continued to pull on clothes, then started gathering a few medical supplies.

"You can't go."

Camille stopped abruptly. "I'm going. I'll face Mama when I get back, so please stop yelling. Tell her that if I help save the major's life, there might be compensation for Charles. We have to try."

Dorothy was on the verge on tears so Camille stopped and touched her arm. "Look, the major saved Katherine and me from a troop of soldiers. I'm not going to refuse to help him. Now pull yourself together and go get some things that I can take to Charles. Hurry."

Dorothy stomped out of the room leaving Camille fuming. She grabbed her medical bag from a dresser, then stuffed a few washed bandages into it.

When Camille entered the parlor wearing trousers and a shirt that couldn't hide a matured body beneath, both soldiers openly stared.

Conscious of their stares, Camille held the bag close to her body. "These are my brother's clothes. It's all I have."

Sergeant Stafford took a couple of seconds to find his voice. "They're just fine."

The ride to the island wasn't extremely bad compared to what she and her family had gone through earlier in the year, but by the time their boat tied up at the pier by the fort, her hair was dripping wet and she was freezing. Everything stuck to her body from the spray, but there was nothing she could do. She pulled her cape around her tighter and hoped most of the soldiers were nowhere near.

Camille followed the sergeant down the wharf and across the loosely put-together boardwalk leading to the fort. She scanned the stockade where hundreds of men huddled together against the fence. Pulling her gaze away from the prisoners, she followed the soldier into the fort, torn between looking for Charles and going directly to Jake.

Sergeant Stafford saw her looking. "I'll arrange for you to see your brother before dark. We'll check the items that you brought him, but we'll let you give them to him yourself."

"Thank you. That's very thoughtful of you."

She followed the sergeant through the familiar entrance of the fort and into the same room where she and her family had slept.

He placed her bags on one of the cots. "We'll put your things here. I assume this is where you'll be staying. It's safe here and you'll be close to the major."

Camille picked up the one bag containing the medicines and walked around the wall. A young man sitting next to the cot stood up and stepped back. Camille took his place by the cot.

Jake lay very still. His ashen face had a heavy two- or three-day beard that couldn't hide the fever-flushed cheeks and the sunken eyes. His chest heaved unevenly. Camille sat in the chair next to him and touched his hand.

"Jake, can you hear me?"

His eyelids fluttered and his head moved slightly. His breath became strained as he struggled to open his eyes.

"Camille," he said in a voice almost inaudible.

"Yes, Jake, I'm here. I brought some medicines that will have you fixed up in no time," she lied. Looking at him told her that it would be a struggle to save his life. He was on fire with fever.

"Sergeant Stafford . . ."

"Please call me Maxwell."

"Certainly. Could you send someone to the end of the pier to get a bucket or two of clean water?"

"There won't be any need for that. We have fresh water from an artesian well."

"No, I want clean, cold saltwater. It's the best thing to clean a wound. We'll use the rest to bathe him down. We need to bring down the fever."

Maxwell left without a word, but returned quickly. "That water will be here shortly," he said as he knelt down by the cot. He helped Camille take off Jake's shirt.

Jake was almost oblivious to what they were doing,

but several times he grabbed her hand. When they lifted him to remove his shirt, his head rolled back. He moaned and his arm went around Camille. He held onto her until she lowered his body back to the cot. Gradually he let go of her and his hands slid back to the sheet.

Jake's shoulder had been bandaged rather awkwardly, but she could tell someone had spent a great deal of time wrapping and rewrapping to make the bandage stay.

Maxwell handed her a pair of scissors. Gently, she cut away the blood-stained strips. Upon removing the last of it, a horrible stench made her turn her head. A black, jagged gash splayed open surrounded by a swollen area, tight and red.

"We're going to need more than just water to clean this out. Do you think you can find me about four sharp knives? Put them in an oven or an open fire. I'll need them hot enough to burn away that layer of infection inside the wound. I've never done it before, but I've helped Mama more than once."

"Do you think it'll work?"

Camille shrugged. "Sometimes it does. Do you think you can help me do it?"

He nodded. "I'll get back as soon as I get those knives in the fire. Lucius will know what to do."

The water was brought in, and Camille wasted no time beginning to wash Jake down. She washed his face and his chest, soaking him with the cold water.

Several times she passed the wet cloth over the gash, letting the water drip in. Jake rolled his head in agony.

Jake was only semiconscious as she continued to bathe him, but several times he whispered her name. Beads of perspiration appeared on his forehead and upper lip.

"Jake, I'm sorry to hurt you like this. I know this salt water burns, but, believe me, it's good for you."

She kissed his forehead, but he didn't respond. She was glad. Not being completely conscious would be a blessing when she inserted the knives into his shoulders. "Please let him pass out quickly," she prayed. "Don't let me hurt him."

She was still bathing his upper body when Maxwell returned.

"Lucius is taking care of the knives. He'll bring them in when they're ready. He said he helped his papa on the plantation do this same thing and will do what you need."

"I'm glad to hear someone else thinks I'm doing the right thing. You never know if you are or not."

Camille held Jake's hand tightly. He rested quietly for the moment, and Camille hated what she was about to do to him.

Lucius and another soldier carried in two bundles of knives.

"What do you want us to do?" asked Maxwell.

"I'll need one of you to hold his shoulders down, one to keep his arms down, and one to keep him from lifting or turning from the hip area." She removed one of the hot knives. The heat made her stomach flip.

"Miss Camille," said Lucius quietly, "I'll do it if you want."

"I'll be okay, but thank you," she said with a half smile. "Just don't be afraid to tell me if I do something wrong."

Jake was being pushed against the cot by three pairs of hands. Camille took a deep breath, tried to steady her hand, and leaned close to Jake. "It'll be over quick," she whispered in his ear.

Afraid that if she thought too long about what she had to do, she would back out, she inserted the flat side of the blade into the wound and pressed it against the side. Immediately Jake's body bolted off the bed and strained against the hands holding him down. A deep groan escaped his lips. His head rolled against the pillow. His body spasmed with pain.

Even though the smell of burning flesh made her weak, Camille held onto the knife steadily. Before removing it, she scraped the edge along the opening of the wound. This time Jake raised his body, jerking and fighting the men holding him, but before he could cause too much damage, his eyes rolled back in his head and his body went limp.

"Thank God," Camille said as the perspiration seeped through her clothing and rolled down her face. With Jake fully unconscious, she was able to finish cleaning the wound with all four hot knives. The men stood back. Before long, she was flushing the area with saltwater and applying the medicines she had brought with her.

When she finished, she stood up. The room spun around her, and she grabbed onto Maxwell's arm for support.

"Here, sit down." He grabbed a clean cloth, dampened it, and placed it on her forehead. "You're white as a ghost. You're not going to faint, are you?"

Camille managed a smile. "No. I always seem to react after the worst is over. I'll be better in a minute."

She looked over at Jake, lying on the bed unconscious. He seemed to be paler now, but his breathing was easier.

"I've got someone coming in to watch the major so you can eat and see your brother," said Maxwell. "Come on. Major Warren will be fine for the little while you're gone."

Camille took one last look at Jake and then let Maxwell lead her out into the other part of the room. "If I could have a few minutes alone, I need to change into a dress. I don't want to upset my brother."

She changed clothes, accepted a plate of food for herself and for Charles as they passed the courtyard oven, then followed the sergeant to the familiar room where they had visited Charles before.

After the initial hug, he held her at arm's length. His deep set frown told her he wasn't pleased. "Are you crazy, little sister? Don't you have enough sense than to come to an island alone? Do you know what you've gotten yourself into?"

"It's not like that at all, Charles."

"Oh, really? Just what is it really like?" he asked sarcastically.

He was much thinner now than at their last visit, and she knew he was having a tough time being there. How could he understand the way the felt about Jake?

"Major Warren saved my life before. I couldn't ignore the opportunity to pay him back. Anyway, Sergeant Stafford and several of the other young men with him have met our family and are very protective. They would never let anything happen to me."

He turned sharply. "You have no idea what these men are capable of."

"Has it been awful for you?" she asked softly.

He faced her. "This is a prison camp. It's not playtime. They're killing us a little at a time with no food, shelters that aren't sufficient, and no medical help. My men live with diarrhea and dysentery. Why haven't they asked you to come help us? You're one of us, not them."

"Listen to yourself." She tried to keep her voice steady and calm, knowing that he was on edge. "We couldn't nurse all of the prisoners out here, nor would you want us to. They asked me as a favor to help the major because, well, I owe him." She couldn't tell her brother how she really felt toward his captor.

"Well, you get yourself off the island as fast as you can. I can't protect you from inside the cages they keep us in."

"You're not in a cage."

"No? Well, what do you call that fence? It feels like a cage when you can't get out. With the sun beating down on you in the summer. With the wind cutting you in the winter."

She went to him and pulled him to her. "I'm so sorry, Charles. I didn't mean to sound like I didn't sympathize with what you're dealing with out here. We pray for you every day. You're always on our minds and in our hearts."

Charles held her desperately close. She could feel the bones through his clothes.

"Don't stay out here. Promise me," he pleaded.

"As soon as I know the major is out of danger, I promise I'll leave."

She calmed him down long enough to eat. He gobbled his plate, then when she offered hers to him, he slowed down a bit and ate hers. Tears formed in his eyes.

"No one should be out here." She voiced her thoughts out loud. "No one should be in any prisoner-of-war camp anywhere."

He placed his hand on her arm. "Just pray for the war to be over soon. We can't survive out here forever."

She kissed him and left with a guard.

With only thin streaks of light left from the setting sun, she was glad to have an escort. Eyes stared at her from behind windows and fences. Haunting eyes that made her uneasy and sad.

Chapter Seven

J ake was resting quietly when Camille returned to the room. His fever still burned, but his breathing seemed more normal. She began to bathe him again with the cold water.

All night she sat by him. He rolled his head from side to side, moaned in his sleep, tried to raise up several times, but was never fully awake. Twice he opened his eyes and seemed to acknowledge her presence, but she wasn't sure if he actually saw her or not.

He talked incoherently all night about what seemed to be home. At one point he said her name, but she was sure he hadn't actually known she was there.

By daybreak, one of the soldiers brought in some coffee.

"Sergeant Stafford asked me to bring this to you. He wanted to make sure you were comfortable."

Camille held the steaming cup up to her nose. "This is wonderful. You know, it's been a long time since I've had real coffee. In fact, the last cup I had was out here in August."

Even with no sugar or milk as she used to drink it before the war, the strong coffee tantalized her taste buds. All of her senses came alive.

She smiled at the young soldier. "Thank you so much, and thank Sergeant Stafford. Tell him Major Warren didn't have a very good night, but he's resting well right now."

He nodded. "Lucius will send in your breakfast. If there's anything else you need, please let me know."

"I need two things. First, I'd like someone to help me shave the major, then I need to get word to my mother that I'm okay."

He nodded. "I think both of those things can be arranged. I know we have a boat going to the mainland this morning. I'll check with the sergeant to make sure word gets to your family."

Jake lay very still. Even though his color seemed a little better since yesterday, his eyes appeared to be sunken even more in his face. She wondered if what they had done for him would do any good.

She leaned over and brushed a lock of hair from his forehead. His skin still burned from the fever. She dipped her cloth and bathed him. Again and again she had to rinse the cloth to keep it cool.

At one point when she placed it on his chest, he grabbed her wrist with his right hand.

"Lie still, Jake. It's me, Camille."

He looked at her through half-closed, glazed eyes. "Millie? Are you really here?" His voice was a weak whisper.

"Yes, Jake. It's me. I've been here since yesterday." She took the opportunity to get him to drink. Cradling his head in her arms, she placed the tin cup to his dry lips, but after only a couple of sips, he grimaced. She lowered him back onto the pillow.

"Stay by me, Millie. Don't leave," he said with his mouth next to her body.

"I'm not leaving, Jake. I'm right here." She kissed his lips gently.

He didn't respond, but relaxed against the pillow and seemed to sleep.

For the remainder of the day, she sat by him. Several times she got him to take more water, but that was the extent of his awareness.

Maxwell came in with a plate of supper for her. "It's late, Miss Camille. Why don't you let me or someone else sit with the major? You need some sleep."

"I won't feel right if I do that. I know his fever will break soon. I'll sleep then. Anyway, I've been dozing on and off in this chair."

Late into the night, she walked to the small opening

in the exterior wall. She knew it was late because she had listened to the men earlier as they talked and laughed and had their card games along the walls of the fort. Now the night was silent.

The tiny window, just large enough for her to see the moon's reflection on the water, framed a cloudless sky with stars that seemed close enough to touch.

She thought about her mother and her sisters and brother and then about Jake. How had life become so confusing? How had she ended up nursing a Union officer on the same island where her brother was being held a prisoner?

How could anyone let a war continue for so long, knowing that situations like this actually happened?

It wasn't right. Nothing seemed right anymore.

The moonlight, the sparkles on the water, the stars—nothing fit in with the situation at all. It was confusing. Upsetting.

She turned to check on Jake. The dim lantern light shining down on his face made him as unbelievable as the peaceful night. He too was confusing, or at least he made life confusing for her. She couldn't believe she'd actually come out here without thinking, without telling anyone but her sisters. At the moment, it seemed like the right thing to do, and she'd do it again if she had to.

She wondered what would happen when she got home. By now she was sure everyone from one end of the coastline to the other knew she had come out here to nurse a Union officer.

How would her friend Michael feel? She was surprised that he hadn't found a boat to get out here.

Her hand flew to her mouth. Surely Michael wouldn't come to an island of Union soldiers. He'd end up in the compound along with all the other soldiers. She couldn't bear to have anything bad happen to her good friend.

She looked at the moon, this time knowing it shone on her family and on Michael back at home. Was he at her house consoling her mother? He was a good man, and now that the war was over for him because of his leg, she prayed that he'd find happiness, but she prayed he didn't want it to be with her. For so long everyone thought they'd end up together, but now, she knew it would never be.

She took a deep breath. "Oh, Michael, why can't I feel toward you as I do this man," she spoke softly.

"Millie?"

She spun around. "Jake, are you awake?" She threw herself down on her knees by his bed. "I'm here. Can you see me?"

"Yes to all of that," he whispered.

After Camille moistened his lips with a wet cloth, he continued, "What are you doing here?" His words came out jerky. His breath uneven.

"I came to take care of you. Your men've been kind to me. Don't try to say any more. You're very weak." She lifted his head for another drink.

He took a sip and closed his eyes.

She pulled a chair close to the bed. "You rest. I'm right here if you need me."

Jake didn't say anything in answer, but feebly reached out and grabbed her hand, drew it to his body, and held it close. Throughout the night, he awakened for a few minutes at a time, reached out for her and squeezed her hand. Sometimes he smiled weakly. Sometimes he only looked at her as if reassuring himself that she was there before lapsing into restless sleep.

She finally placed her head against his, and they both slept peacefully.

When she opened her eyes around dawn, he was looking at her with conscious recognition. The smile he gave was real.

"Good morning," she said and tried to lift her head, but he pulled her close to him.

"Don't go."

"Your fever's broken. Maybe you'd rest better if I went in the other room."

Shaking his head, he turned her hand over in his, then smiled. "It feels right having you here." He looked down at their hands. "We fit together," he said with a weak voice.

Camille couldn't find the words to tell him how wrong he was. She knew they could never fit together in the world that they found themselves in.

For a long time, Camille sat in the dimness of the room, listening to his breathing, watching the rise and fall of his chest.

For two days she had been by him as a nurse, but tonight she stayed by him as something much more. It was a night she would treasure always, because in the light of the morning, there couldn't be anything between them. Ever.

Once Jake's fever broke, his recovery was quick. By the afternoon, he sat up on the side of the cot and ate a light soup fixed by Lucius just for him. By the next morning, he got out of bed.

"What are you doing up?" Camille hurried into the room.

"I can't stay in bed forever. I have a prison camp to run, remember?"

"Certainly I remember, but I also remember that you have a hole in your shoulder and a good chance of getting it infected again if you don't take care of yourself."

"I think I've been taken care of pretty good. I've had an angel by my side," he said with a wink.

Neither of them mentioned the night she'd stayed next to him or the fact that he'd kissed her. She told herself it was the fever that made him reach out to her.

"I don't know about an angel, but you've had a parade of wonderful men taking care of you and running the camp for you. Your men are very loyal, Major Warren."

"We're back to being Major Warren, huh?" He

reached for his shirt. "Here, help me with this, Nurse Hollander."

She laughed. It was good to see him strong enough to joke.

Camille held the shirt as he slipped his right arm into the sleeve, then turned around for her to put the left side of the shirt just over the shoulder.

As she turned, she found herself looking directly up into his eyes. She held onto the shirt for a second unable to move, then pretended to be occupied with securing it.

Very slowly, he lifted his hand and placed it over hers. She stopped, held her breath, and dared not to move.

"Jake, I have to leave. You know that."

He pulled her to his chest. "I've thought of nothing else since my fever broke. You have to leave, and you have to leave this morning. You've been here too long."

She was crushed. Surprised at her reaction to something that she knew was true, she tried to smile.

"Yes, I'm sure my family is frantic. I sent word, but they won't understand."

She tried to pull away, but he held her close. "You shouldn't have come out here alone, but you know that I'm grateful. I'm more than grateful," he whispered.

She tried to act casual. "You helped my sister and me on the road that day. I didn't think twice about coming."

"Is that the only reason you came?"

Her breath caught in her throat. She turned away from him, embarrassed that he'd know she struggled with feelings that could never be. "Why wouldn't it be?"

"Because ever since I met you, I've thought about you. You're different, Camille, different from the other girls I've met down here . . ."

Camille pulled away from him. Hurt and embarrassed, she stood with her shoulders back and her head high.

"Different?" She pushed aside the hurt. Her temper flared. "Different because I have to wear faded dresses, fish for my family, and dry salt every waking hour of the day, not to mention digging bullets out of enemy soldiers?"

She spun around and paced the floor. "Is that what makes me different?" She fought back tears. "Major, I used to be a lady just like all those females you're used to being with like Mrs. Darcey's Mary Elizabeth, but you and your Union put an end to that . . ."

Jake grabbed her by her arms. She turned into his embrace, but seeing a smile on his face, she pulled away again. He grabbed his shoulder, then sat on the side of the bed.

Instantly, she put her arm around him for support. "I'm sorry. I didn't mean to hurt you. I should've never gotten into this conversation."

It took Jake a minute to find the strength to answer

her. "Camille, I'm not making fun of your situation. I said you're different and you didn't give me time to finish. I happen to like what I see." His words were jerky. His breath jagged. "I admire you for what you do. I was trying to give you a compliment."

"Don't." She tried to spit the word out, make it sound mean and strong, but it didn't. It came out soft and low. Confused, she knew she had to leave. *He's North. I'm South*, she reminded herself. "I'm going to find Sergeant Stafford, then I really do need to go."

"Don't go mad. Please, Millie. Sit with me for a minute."

All of her instincts told her to leave, for the longer she stayed near him, the harder it would be to say good-bye.

His face still showed the ravages of pain, but a tiny curl of his lip showed his pleasure of being with her. How could she deny him?

Reluctantly, she sat on the cot next to him. He didn't try to touch her. In fact, he didn't even look at her.

"You've saved my life. We're even. I hope we don't have to be indebted to each other again." This time he looked at her with longing. "You are I are different, and no matter how hard we would try, we'll always be. Your brother is my prisoner. There's nothing we can do about that."

"You could let him go," she interrupted.

"No, I can't. You know that. I have my job to do

and whether I believe every order that I follow is right, I have to do as my rank requires. This is wartime." He turned toward her. "It's war, but it will be over soon, I know it."

"And you'll return to Rhode Island . . ."

"How did . . . ?"

"Sergeant Stafford mentioned your home."

"Yes, I'll return to Rhode Island for a time at least," he swallowed before he continued, "and you and your family will be able to rebuild your lives. That's the way it is."

Nothing had been said about a future together, but she knew what he was saying. It was what she'd told herself over and over. There could never be anything between them.

"I thought I could walk you out to the boat, but I don't think I have the strength." He turned and placed both hands on her arms. "Will you kiss me good-bye?"

"I shouldn't," she said, but was leaning into his arms as the words slipped out.

Her lips met his with a longing she never knew existed, not just a physical longing, but a longing for more from life than this moment in time allotted her. She didn't want to leave him or return to the drudgery of trying to survive while the South languished in their last efforts. His was a kiss of farewell, and it broke her heart.

Jake ended the kiss and pulled her to him. There

was no movement from him, only the rhythmic quivers from his breathing and the pounding of his heart.

This was good-bye. They both knew it.

"Forgive me. I shouldn't have done that. That was supposed to be only a sweet good-bye kiss."

"There's nothing to forgive. I've never been kissed like that," she said unembarrassed. "I'll remember it always, and I'll always remember you."

He stared into her eyes for a long time. "You know that in another time and another place, we wouldn't be saying good-bye. I'd be making plans to court you, take you to balls and picnics, and making plans for a future with you."

"Jake, don't say things like that. It makes it harder to leave."

"I want you to know the truth. I don't want you to go, but you have to."

"I know."

He smiled. "I want you to remember me, but remember me with a smile." He winked at her as she turned to go. "Times will change, you'll see."

She wasn't sure how to respond to that, but she knew she had to go while she could. "Good-bye, Jake, and please find it in your heart to take care of my brother."

Without looking back, she followed Sergeant Stafford out of the fort and out of Jake Warren's life.

Chapter Eight

Several months passed since Camille and Major Warren said their good-byes. She returned home to rumors and accusing looks from her neighbors. Helping the returning wounded kept her busy, and even though their families accepted her medical attention, they turned a deaf ear to her explanations of why she had gone to the island.

Salt barrels had been abandoned and her sisters took over the job of fishing. She missed being out on the water alone where she could forget the reality of life on shore.

One warm February morning, her mother volunteered to make the rounds alone so Camille could help her sisters. Camille hummed as she readied the boat, but before she could push away from the dock, Joseph rowed to the pier informing her Mrs. Darcey needed her once more.

Assuming Mr. Darcey was ill, but hating to abandon her sisters again, she reluctantly grabbed her meager medical supplies and climbed into the boat with Joseph.

"And you have no idea why she wants me, Joseph?"

"No, ma'am," he said as he rowed. "She just said to go get Ms. Hollander."

"But are you sure she wanted me and not Mother?"

Joseph heaved a deep breath and repeated once more. "Yes, ma'am. She said to bring back the young Ms. Hollander."

Camille sat on the boat's front bench, stumped at why Mrs. Darcey would want to see her instead of her mother, but she knew it wouldn't do any good to question Joseph any more. She tried to relax and enjoy the warm morning sun.

As they approached the channel that led to the open water, she tried not to look south. Ship Island lay twelve miles out, not in her view, but definitely in her mind and in her heart.

Lying in her bed at night alone, she was unable to control her thoughts and her dreams. Over and over she relived the days she'd sat by Jake's side as he recuperated. The memories bore into her heart with the kind of ache she'd never felt before.

Making herself look away from the south channel, she folded her hands on her lap and stared straight ahead. A job awaited her at the Darceys'—or at least she thought it did—and that would help her forget. Keeping busy had gotten her through the last few years of this war and it would help her get through the remainder of it. But even as she said those words, she knew that things would be forever changed for her.

Never had she felt the pull to be with someone as she had with the major. Would she ever feel that way toward anyone else again? Why couldn't she feel that way about Michael? She felt guilty when she returned from the island and saw how upset and concerned he was. Now he was much more attentive and obviously more caring. She prayed her feelings for him could grow beyond friendship. She didn't want to hurt her friend.

"Miss Camille, you need to hold on while I get this line tied good and tight."

Camille had been in such deep thought she hadn't realized Joseph had eased the boat up to the Darcey pier. He tied the stern rope, then ambled up to the front and secured that one.

He placed her bag on the pier, then helped her out of the boat.

She headed toward the back door instead of the front porch, expecting Mrs. Darcey to greet her in her usual welcome, but she didn't. She assumed no one had seen the boat near the property.

As soon as she knocked, Alice opened the door, then stepped aside. "Come in, Miss Camille. I'll be in the front of the house if you need something."

Camille opened her mouth to question where everyone was when she caught movement by the hall door. She dropped her bag and grabbed the door facing. "Jake."

Jake stepped into the kitchen. Dressed in his uniform pants, but wearing a white shirt opened at the neck, he took her breath away.

"Hello, Camille. I hope you don't mind that I'm here."

For several moments, Camille struggled to catch her breath before answering.

"Why are you here? Is something wrong?" She held on tighter. "Oh, my God. Has something happened to Charles?"

Jake took several long steps toward her and took her arms. "No, no. Nothing is wrong. In fact, everything is good."

Camille closed her eyes to let what he said sink in. "So Charles is okay? And you? Has your shoulder healed?"

He nodded. "We're both okay." His words came out a little less than enthusiastic.

"But not good."

"We're both surviving. I'm almost back to normal. A few aches still, but okay, I guess. Charles is okay as well, but he's in a prisoner-of-war camp on an island. His life could be better."

"Of course," she answered, took a deep breath, then looked him in the eyes. "So, why are you at the

Darceys'? Are they having their company in from Mobile again?"

Jake grinned. "No, no company. I'm it." He cleared his throat. "I asked Mrs. Darcey if she'd mind if I used her house as a meeting place. I wanted to see you again."

"Jake," she hesitated, feeling her heart flutter at his confession, "I thought we agreed we shouldn't see each other again."

"We did, but, well, I had to see you." He smiled, stepped toward the table, then placed his hand on a large picnic basket. "I wanted to do something normal, and fun, with you. I know this sounds idiotic, but you don't know me. You've only seen me in my official role as an enemy officer. I wanted you to know there was a real person under that uniform."

"We're going to have a picnic?"

He nodded.

"A picnic in the middle of a war?"

"Well, there's not a lot of shooting going on down here."

She smiled with him. "I'd love to have a picnic."

"I brought a few things from the island, and Mrs. Darcey took care of the rest. There's enough to call it a picnic."

He picked up the basket with one hand and placed his other on her waist. Together they walked into the backyard.

"I thought we'd go down by the bay under that big

oak tree. It's away from the main channel, but close to the house."

Camille understood. Too many boats passed in front of the house, and even though there was good rapport between the soldiers on the island the locals, feelings were heightened now that it was evident the South could never win.

The winter sun warmed them as they walked down the sloping lawn to a shady spot under the tree where Jake spread a blanket. She bent down and started taking items from the basket. When she got to the bread, she held it up. "This is from Lucius, isn't it?"

"Yes, he said to tell you he worked extra hard with it this morning, just for you."

"Tell him I send my thanks." She inhaled and closed her eyes. "When I smell this, I can almost feel the warm island air and hear the wind blowing across the sand. Your island might be a prison right now, but it's a beautiful spot." She smiled.

"And your smile is beautiful. You need more to smile about."

Embarrassed, she reached in and took out a small knife and two plates along with two metal cups.

He placed a finger on her chin. She froze as he lifted her face. "Don't turn away from me. I like to see you smile. That's the way I want to remember you."

His eyes, deep blue with a hint of sadness, bore into hers. She wanted to tell him that he didn't need to remember her if they were together, but she knew that could never be.

She pulled away.

"And I thank you for remembering my smile and not a muddy girl on the road to New Orleans."

This time he laughed out loud. "Oh, but I won't forget that sight either. You can't imagine the picture you presented that day. Fuming mad. Defiant. But about as beautiful a picture as I've ever seen."

"And you, Major Warren, shouldn't fib like that. Maybe mad and a little out of control, but beautiful?" She shook her head and laughed. "Oooh, I can still feel all that mud stuck on me and in my hair. The next day it was worse."

"Did I ever apologize for what those soldiers did?"

She stopped digging through the basket and looked up again. "No, I don't think you have."

"On behalf of the entire Union Army," he said with overexaggerated drama, "I do apologize." And then he got serious. "And for not being able to help you more."

Camille reached back into the basket and took out a cloth wrapped around a small piece of dried meat. "You did what you could."

"Maybe, but I wanted to do more."

"Katherine and I survived, but it's a moment in my life best forgotten." She looked up. "But this is a moment I'd like to remember."

She placed food on his plate and then on hers. As she handed him a cup of water, their hands touched, reminding her that Jake Warren was warm and human and caring. He had taken time out of his life to be with her.

He looked from their hands to her eyes. Nothing was said, but what she read in his eyes told her the depth of his emotions reached far deeper than he would ever admit.

She pulled her hand back, settled down on the blanket, and together they ate in familiar silence. When they finished, he helped her repack their basket, then he stretched out on the blanket and looked up at the tree limbs.

"Thank you, Jake," Camille said as she sat on her side of the blanket. "This felt almost real."

"This was real, Camille."

"No, it wasn't. This was pretend. We pretended the war didn't exist. That you weren't the enemy. That my brother wasn't your prisoner, and that you and I could actually do this in public one day."

His chest heaved. His face got serious. "Maybe we did pretend, but wasn't it worth it? You deserve to have a little joy in your life. I was trying to do that for you." He stopped and swallowed. "And I wanted your thoughts of me to be more than that mean commander at the island."

"I could never remember you like that, you know that."

"I hope that's true."

Camille pulled her knees up to her chin and stared out at the water. "I know we're losing this war. How long will you be here after it's over?"

"I don't know." He turned on his side and propped his head up with his hand. "I guess we'll process the prisoners out, and I'll report back to Washington. I'm not really sure how long it will take."

"Then you'll go to Rhode Island?"

He nodded.

"Do you have someone waiting for you?"

A grin spread across his face. "I hope not."

That brought a chuckle from Camille. "What does that mean?"

"This girl, uh, Sarah Jenkins, and I have been friends for a long time. Our families decided a long time ago we'd make a good union. Her dad is my dad's partner at the bank. They just never thought about asking me about it though."

"And Sarah? What does she think about the arrangement?"

"Who knows. We wrote a couple times since I enlisted, but I think I made it clear I didn't want her waiting for me. Maybe she got the hint and found her a beau."

Camille nodded and rested her head on her knees. "What's she like?"

He looked at her a long time before answering. "Not like you at all."

"I see." She said with a quiet voice.

"No, I doubt you do. She's blonde and beautiful—but not as beautiful as you. Her parents sent her to finishing school."

Camille thought about Mary Elizabeth and the type of girls like her from New Orleans and Mobile. That was probably what Sarah Jenkins was like.

"I guess she's pretty smart," Jake continued, "but I wonder if she could do the things that you've done to keep your family alive."

"She would. I don't know your Sarah, but most women do what needs to be done when the occasion arises. War just happened to make me do things I never thought I'd do before."

"But you did them and didn't complain."

Camille laughed. "You haven't been around me very long, Major Warren. I complain a lot. I complain about the faded clothes I have to wear, about fishing instead of sleeping late, about not having the means to help the soldiers who come home wounded." She looked at her hands. "And I complain about these leathery hands from working the salt barrels."

Jake sat up, then reached over and took both of her hands into his. "I'm not complaining about those hands. They saved my life, in case you've forgotten."

He pulled them up to his lips and kissed them. Camille closed her eyes and relished the warmth and peace that flowed through her. How she wished their time together wouldn't end and his kisses would go on for a lifetime.

But it wasn't so and never would be. She pulled her hand back.

"Thank you. You make me feel like a lady when you do things like that."

"That's because you are a lady, Camille. A beautiful, resourceful lady who'll make some man a wonderful wife."

"But not your wife." Her hands flew up to her mouth. "I'm sorry. I shouldn't have said that."

Jake studied her. "That's another reason I think you're so wonderful. You say what you think." He took her hand again. "If times were different . . ."

"But they're not. We are who we are. We can't change that, no matter how much I'd like to."

He brought her hands back up to his lips once more. "Times will change and neither of us knows what the future holds."

Chapter Nine

The first few months of 1865 stayed mild and quietly turned into the springlike days of March, but for Camille and the other villagers, life hadn't gotten any better.

From the news that trickled down to the coast, they knew the South was losing, and by March it was clear the war would be over shortly. News of Lee and Grant's meeting at Appomattox reached them the second week in April. It was almost a relief.

With more and more men returning to their homes, food and supplies of any kind were in even shorter supply. The Hollander women, including Katherine and Dorothy, devoted their entire days to helping the soldiers. Several men from the front beach in Biloxi de-

livered mullet to the family regularly so their family
and others around them could eat.

Michael became a presence in Camille's life, pro-
viding as much food and help as he could with one
leg, but he didn't try to hide his dislike of her being
on the road constantly.

Camille sensed his agitation and reminded him
she'd also nursed him. She tried hard not to lead
him on, but he insisted on helping her family. He'd
just smile and kiss her lightly on the cheek. "Things
will work out, Millie. You'll see."

Camille worried things wouldn't work out for them.
She loved Michael as a friend, and still prayed that
their relationship would grow beyond friendship. He
was pleasant and kind, and he was here.

Jake Warren had vanished from her life, and she
worked to do the same with his memories. With the
war over, she had to move on.

But even with the fighting officially over, Charles
had not returned. Someone in the neighborhood
stayed close to their home in case her brother came
home without warning.

By the middle of April, they began to worry.

Coming home from church one Sunday, Camille
spotted a boat in the bay. She was certain it was from
the island.

"Mama, look!" She lifted the front of her dress
and ran across the lawn. As she stopped at the water's

edge, the others caught up with her, waving and shouting to the boat, but Camille saw right away that there were no Confederate uniforms in the boat. Something was wrong.

The first person she recognized was Major Jake Warren, sitting in the back of the boat alone. Anger shot through her. She had struggled constantly to keep him out of her mind. Recently it had been working, but now seeing him in person renewed emotions she didn't want to face. How could he do this?

Then she panicked. He would never come see her just for a visit. Trying to keep her mind from thinking the worst, she stood rigid, unmoving, trying to let the anger at seeing him override the fear of why he was here.

Her hands unconsciously grabbed the sides of her skirt, twisting the fabric around her fingers. Mrs. Hollander and the girls were still ecstatic, and her heart went out to them.

The boat pulled up alongside the pier and two men jumped out in front of Jake. He jumped up next, gave some orders to the men, then walked alone to the group of women who now stood solemn.

Camille's heart ached as she watched him walk down the pier toward them. The magnetism was still there. Confusion set in once more as his blue eyes sought her out, making her feel as if no one else was on the lawn. She saw him and nothing else.

His eyes never wavered from hers as he walked

down the planks until Mrs. Hollander ran up to him. He tipped his hat to her.

"Ladies, I'd like to speak to you. I'm sorry to come unannounced, but there's something I wanted to tell you personally." Jake's strained look told her that the news wasn't good.

Mrs. Hollander's hand went up to her mouth. Jake reached out and steadied her. He looked over at Camille then back to Mrs. Hollander. "It hurts me to have to tell you this, but your son, Captain Hollander, got in a scuffle with one of my guards yesterday and was shot. He died instantly."

Mrs. Hollander let out a deep moan, and Dorothy and Katherine grabbed her.

Camille watched the blood drain from her mother's face. Her own stomach knotted. Her head felt light.

"How can that be?" she asked in a voice that she didn't recognize. "The war's over. Why wasn't he just sent home? How could your men kill him?"

Jake stepped near her and pulled his hand across his chin. "We were processing the prisoners out, but it was slow and tedious. They had to be transported to Vicksburg to be paroled or pardoned. Captain Hollander and his company would've been on the next ship."

Mrs. Hollander's sob cut him off. He swallowed hard before continuing.

"I don't know what happened to your son, ma'am. He'd become agitated and started acting strange over the past few weeks. Maybe Lee's surrender drove him to it. I don't know, but he wasn't himself. My guard couldn't take any chances. He said he tried to subdue him, but Charles tried to take the weapon from him. Pulling the trigger was all he could do."

Camille's body trembled.

Jake looked at Camille. "I'm so sorry. I am. I was with him when he died. He never regained consciousness. He didn't suffer."

"Where's my son's body?" asked Mrs. Hollander in a flat monotone.

Jake pulled his eyes away from Camille. "We have him ready for burial. Another boat is coming in behind us. If you'll allow us, we'll dig a grave or do whatever else there is to do."

"No," Mrs. Hollander spit out. "You've done enough. Go. Leave my family alone. I don't want you here when Charles comes home."

"Mama, please. This man didn't take Charles' life."

"Didn't he, Camille? He and all the other Yankees are responsible for this." She turned and led her other two daughters into the house.

Camille stood by Jake. "This is more horrible than being killed in battle."

"I agree, but Camille, I swear, there was nothing we did to provoke this. Charles lost control. He wasn't the same."

"Why didn't you come get us? Maybe we could've helped him."

Jake stepped near her. Camille could tell he wanted to reach out to her. She stepped away.

"I thought about it often," he said, "but I couldn't bring myself to see you again."

"So you let my brother's mind waste away. Wasn't that a little selfish?"

Jake nodded. "He was a prisoner, just like all the hundreds of others."

"No, he wasn't. He was my only brother. My mother's only son."

Jake swallowed hard. "I'm sorry. I really am."

"You need to go. Seeing you here will make it worse for Mother when his body arrives."

"And what about for you, Camille? Will my presence make it worse for you?"

His words made her breath catch in her throat. How could he ask her such a question when she was sure he knew the answer?

"I'm fine. You can't stay any longer."

"You're lying, but I'll go, if you think it best."

"It's the only way," she said under her breath. She looked up to him and without warning, tears flooded her eyes. Jake was suffering as much as she was. He didn't take his job or his men lightly, and for that he was in pain and would always be even after the war was over. His pain was as real as hers.

"Jake, I'm sorry for you too. I know this isn't how you wanted all this to end, but the war is over. You can return to Rhode Island. We'll still be here to face no telling what from the federal government."

He grabbed her arms and spun her around. "Do you think my life will all of a sudden become a bed of roses just because the war is over? You're wrong, terribly wrong, if you do. Sure, I'll be going home. In fact, as soon as I have the prisoners returned, I'll be requesting a transfer. I hope to be gone by June, but this place'll always be with me. Things happened out there on that island and on the battlefields that will stay with me always. Charles' death will be at the top of the list."

Camille stood inches away from Jake, confused as she'd never been before. The piece of ground they stood on would be in limbo now that the South had lost. Her brother's body was being rowed home for burial by Union soldiers, and her family would once more have to deal with another tragedy. But in spite of all that, Jake's presence calmed her. She needed him to open his arms and hold her. Longed for his strength, if only for a moment. Just until the world stopped spinning out of control.

But it could never happen. "You need to leave our home," she whispered.

It was a long moment before she felt him move. She looked up. His eyes devoured her, pierced her soul, held her heart. She knew he understood.

"I'm going, Camille, but it isn't what I want to do." He turned to leave, took a few steps, then turned back to her. Her heart stopped, waiting for him to say something, anything, to make the situation more bearable.

He nodded slightly, then hurried to the boat. As it pulled away, their gazes locked until the boat turned south.

Once more, she watched Jake Warren step out of her life.

Chapter Ten

July 1865

Jake Warren looked over three bags of his personal belongings. It was shortly after daybreak, but he'd been up for several hours anticipating his departure at midmorning. For the entire night, he'd tossed and turned, torn with wanting to leave the island to get back to civilization, but dreading leaving behind part of his heart.

The last of the prisoners had been sent to Vicksburg over a month ago to be paroled or exchanged, and since that time he and the remaining troops fought boredom waiting for their official transfer.

It had been a long month. Not having anything to do gave him too much time to think, and his thoughts always returned to Camille. He'd wrestled with his feelings. Going back to Rhode Island wasn't his first choice, but he was smart enough to know he couldn't stay here. No matter how much he dreamed of a life with Camille, he'd never be accepted, especially after the death of Captain Hollander.

Taking the man's body back to his family had been one of his hardest wartime duties. Other soldiers could have delivered the body, but it was an assignment he had to do himself. Charles Hollander wasn't just any Confederate officer. He was Camille's brother. Thinking about the pain and suffering she and her family endured because of his death tore at his heart.

Now he'd have to live with the fact that he'd died under his command, and Camille's family blamed him. Camille understood. He saw it in her eyes, but worse still, he saw more than an understanding of his feelings. As he stood on her back lawn, he'd felt from her the same love and yearning that tormented him.

He cursed the war. Because of who they were, he and Camille now lived with more than the physical scars of battle. The only thing he could think of was getting away from Ship Island and the Mississippi Gulf Coast. Every time he looked north and saw the distant outline of the coast, he ached for something he could never have, and the only way to avoid the hurt was to leave.

"Sir." A young private cleared his throat.

Jake looked up.

"Admiral Buckley sent word that we can begin loading."

"My things are ready. I have a few details left. I'll catch the last boat out to the ship."

"Yes, sir. I'll see that your bags get on board safely." The man turned to leave, then turned back again. "Sir?"

Jake faced him. "Yes?"

"I, uh, just want to say that I've enjoyed serving under you. My tour on the island wasn't the greatest, but you've been excellent. You made it bearable."

"Thank you, Baker. I'm not going to miss much from this experience out here, but I will miss some of you men. You've been out here as long as I have, haven't you?"

"Yes, sir. It's been quite a while." He smiled and turned again to go.

Jake watched the young private leave, then once more looked at that part of the fort that had become his home, or at least his refuge from the drudgery of life out here. He had become familiar with each brick-and-mortar crack as he lay in bed alone each night.

He looked at the stripped cot waiting for the new troops of engineers who would soon man the island. Everything around him reminded him of Camille, but the cot held special memories. He still felt her presence from when she'd nursed him. Heard her whisper his name close to his face. Felt her warm lips on his skin.

She had saved his life, but had stolen his heart.

Abruptly, he put on his dress jacket, put out his cigarette, and walked out. Camille's memory would be tucked away with the few pleasantries from his stay there. She'd be among the sunsets and sunrises, the gentle breezes that blew across the island, and the moonlight glistening on the water.

This barren strip of sand offered little enjoyment, but Camille was a moment in his life that would stay with him forever.

The *Maritime*, the eighteen-gun sloop of war, lay about a half mile from the beach. Her tall masts swayed gently with the swells. Jake smiled as he boarded the transport. At least he wouldn't have to fight rough seas on his last boat ride away from the island. He looked down and brushed away the white grains of sand that clung to his uniformed legs even as he sat in the boat. It would probably be the last time he'd ever have to do that.

Admiral Vernon Buckley was waiting for Jake when he stepped on board.

"Welcome aboard, Jake. It's been a long time." The admiral held out his hand. "You're looking good."

Jake stepped back and raised an eyebrow. "Can't say the same for you. Look at that gut on you."

Buckley put his hands on his belly and roared. "Sitting on a ship for the last three years will do that to you. Come on in and let's catch up on old times." He led Jake into the admiral's cabin, a cabin familiar to Jake with its tightly stacked shelves piled high with every type of published work available.

"You still haven't cleaned the place, have you?"

"If I do, I won't be able to find anything." He poured a mug of wine for each of them.

Jake hadn't been on the ship fifteen minutes and he realized he felt like a different man. The wine warmed his insides, and the ship and Vernon did the rest.

"What are you grinning about?" asked Vernon as he took a sip.

"Nothing. Absolutely nothing. I'm just feeling good to be off that island."

"I was going to suggest we go up on deck and watch the island 'til it's out of sight. As much as you disliked your stay out here, I'm sure you'll miss something about it. Come on. Bring your drink, and let's watch that part of your life disappear."

"Now that's something I'll drink to."

Together they reemerged on deck as the boat was rounding the bend of the island's western point. Fort Massachusetts lay silently in the distance with its massive round walls outlined against the morning sky.

Jake sipped his wine and said nothing. The ten-minute ride out to the ship had taken him away from another lifetime that at that moment seemed not to have ever existed. He would gladly forget about those walls and the sand and the sea and all that it represented.

"You look deep in thought," Vernon interrupted him.

"Just thinking. It's hard to believe it's really ended." He looked on deck and most of the men who'd served with him were also leaning on the railing silently watching the island fade into the distance.

"Just feel lucky that you weren't in the trenches for the whole war like some of the men were."

"Believe me, I do thank the heavens for that small favor. As miserable as this place was, I know the suffering I escaped by being out here."

By sunup the next morning, the *Maritime* pulled into port at New Orleans. They would spend a full week there before heading east along the coast of the Gulf of Mexico and up the Atlantic, picking up some men and dropping off others. Jake hadn't the slightest idea how long the journey home to Rhode Island would take, but he really didn't care.

As he walked down the gangplank, the sights and smells of the city engulfed him. Several years had passed since he'd been stationed there under General Butler, and he had only visited once since then.

He stopped in midtrack. That was the visit when he'd met Camille. Shaking his head, he tried to concentrate on other things. He had to get her out of his thoughts and out of his heart.

He stared out the window of the carriage. The riverfront looked as active as ever with more freed slaves hustling about moving cargo on and off ships and stacking large crates in what seemed to be no order at all. Others lay against the sides of buildings as if in expectation of something to happen. Jake guessed they had come down from the plantations in the northern parts of the neighboring states looking for employment. He wondered what would happen to them and all the other freed slaves up and down the Confederate states.

"You still heading for Pearl's?" asked Vernon as the two of them left the boardinghouse several hours later.

Maybe visiting Pearl's Palace would help pull the curtain down over the scenes that kept playing over and over in his head, but he knew it wasn't what he needed. "No, I think I'll settle down in my room, then grab a bite to eat."

Vernon tilted his head and scrunched his mouth. "You sick or something?"

Jake laughed. "No, just tired." He patted his friend on the back. "You tell Pearl and her girls I said hello, but they'll have to manage without me tonight."

"I'll do it, but are you sure you're feeling well?"

Jake chuckled. "I'm great, now go."

Vernon hopped out of the carriage as soon as it pulled up in front of the establishment, waved to his friend, and headed up the tall steps with a spring in his walk.

Maybe I am sick, Jake thought to himself, not believing he turned down a night at Pearl's.

After giving the carriage driver instructions to take him back to the boardinghouse, he loosened his collar and relaxed against the velvet seat. The night air was heavy. The island had offered a breeze most nights, but here among the buildings the air hung still and lifeless, giving no relief from the sultry summer.

He rubbed his hand along the cool velvet. Except for his occasional trips to the Darcey home, there had been too few times he'd experienced the niceties of life.

His thoughts moved from the Darcey estate to the modest home across the bay and to Camille. Would he ever get the girl out of his mind?

Jake breathed deeply and hoped that the relaxed atmosphere in the postwar city would filter into his body. He was home free. Leaving a barren island. Reporting to Washington for final assignments. Going back to Rhode Island to get the ball rolling on a new career once he signed his discharge papers.

He had the world open to him, but nothing seemed right. His body and his heart were out of sorts, and the tension he felt permeated every part of his being.

The carriage pulled up to the boardinghouse, but instead of going in, he went next door to the Taloux house where Camille had stayed before. The light still shone in the parlor. He knocked.

Mr. Taloux opened the door. "All our rooms are taken. Is there something else I can help you with, monsieur?"

"Yes, sir. My name is Major Jake Warren. I'm staying next door. You had a visitor here last year, and I was wondering if you've heard any news of her family recently. The young lady's name is Camille Hollander, and—"

Mr. Taloux cut him off. "Oh, come on in. Camille was here just last week doing some trading. She had a friend with her. A young man. A soldier I'm sure because he was missing a leg. She didn't stay long, but she looked good. She's such a pretty gal. You know her?"

Jake's interest sharpened at the mention of a man. His chest tightened. "I do. You said she had a young man with her. A friend?"

Mr. Taloux smiled. "Uh, I couldn't say if he was just a friend or if he was a beau. They didn't give me any indication. Had separate rooms."

The pressure lessened. "Did she say how her family was?"

He shook his head. "Real sad situation, I'm afraid. Her mother came down with yellow fever about two months ago and passed, poor soul. One of her sisters went inland to live with an aunt's family. Their brother was killed in that prison camp on Ship Island. Horrible situation. The war had already ended. Horrible situation. Just horrible."

Jake rubbed his hand across the bottom of his face. "Yes, I'd heard about the brother. I agree. It certainly was sad. Why didn't all the sisters leave the coast?"

"Camille said something about taking care of the soldiers coming home. Wanted to start a business too. Can you imagine? A pretty young lady like that starting her own business. Her youngest sister, Katherine, stayed with her."

Jake lifted his eyebrow and chuckled under his breath. "A business, huh? I'm not surprised. What kind of business?"

"Something about fishing supplies. Said since the war, all kinds of Northerners with money were coming to the area and she meant to find a way to make the best of the situation."

Jake chuckled again. "That's Camille." He shook the man's hand before leaving.

It didn't take him long to decide how he'd spend his week before the ship pulled out of port. He had to ride to Biloxi. If there was a man in Camille's life now, the situation would be even better. He could close the door on what never could have been. Just knowing that she was okay, he could return to Rhode Island and get on with his life.

But even as the thoughts materialized in his head, he knew he was kidding himself. Moving on without her would be harder than living on the island knowing that she was just beyond a small body of water.

He cursed the war. Cursed the differences that kept him and Camille apart. Dreaded the long ride on Moses to see her, but already felt her in his arms.

Forget the young man that was with her. He had to hold her once again.

Chapter Eleven

Exhausted, Camille eased down in her mother's favorite old rocker on the porch. Every day more men came home from the prison camps and from the hospitals. They all needed care. Without her mother, she tended them alone or had Katherine at her side, which zapped her of every ounce of energy by the time she got back to her house in the evenings.

When the state had finally surrendered its forces several months back, Camille hoped life would get better for her and Katherine. It hadn't. She watched as the locals moved out of the area searching for someplace they could grow food. Watched as young men were carried home on stretchers or families waited endless hours for their loved ones to return. Some never would.

Fewer than four hundred people remained along the coastline in Biloxi, but even those numbers felt like thousands when food and medicine were short.

Had it not been for the oysters, shrimp, and fish, Camille knew the villagers would not have survived. Michael's father, Mr. Rice, traded wood from his small lumber mill for eggs and vegetables with a farmer from north of the Bay area, but even that was scarce.

After working in the mill all day, Michael and his father fished until sundown for their family and for her, but Camille could tell that the extra work was taking its toll on Michael. His leg hadn't completely healed, and each day she sensed he pushed himself more and more to keep his family and her with food on the table.

Michael was a godsend. He took care of her as if he were her husband, but asked nothing in exchange. He begged her and Katherine to move into his family's home, but she refused. She didn't want him to get the wrong idea about their relationship, so she stayed in her own house. It had always been her home. She felt safe there and close to her family.

Gradually, Mr. Rice stockpiled lumber for her. One day she would pay him for it, but for now he simply cut extra wood every so often and placed it aside for her to construct a building at the end of her pier. It would house a small tackle business of some sorts. She wasn't sure what it would be specifically, but she knew it would take advantage of the waterfront location.

She had even invited Michael to help her run it if it ever got built. He could be a partner, and a male figure present in the business would satisfy the locals and would be something he could do with one leg. She tried to explain the friendly partnership, but she was sure he had other ideas.

Michael pulled up in a borrowed buggy as she was still resting on the porch.

As soon as he got down from the buggy, Camille knew that something was wrong. "Come sit by me."

He struggled with the steps more than usual, but because he always wanted to do it alone, Camille didn't help him. He sat next to her after a brief kiss on the cheek.

"What's wrong, Michael? It's so late for you to be out."

He leaned his head back against the chair and closed his eyes. "You'd think now that the war's over, we'd get some kind of reprieve. They just won't leave us alone. They're going to drain us until the last one of us puts a gun to our heads."

"Stop talking like that. You're scaring me. What in the world happened?"

"Melvin at Handsboro's mill came by today to see if we had a piece of equipment he could borrow. He was upset. Said he'd probably have to sell his place, that is, if he can find a buyer."

"What do you mean sell? I thought he had a good business, and with all this construction that's bound to take place since the war's over, he'll make a fortune."

"He will if he still has the business, but most people just trade goods for his lumber right now. No one has money and his taxes are due next month. He showed me the notice. Camille, his taxes are enormous. There's no way he can come up with that amount on either the house or his mill. He was in such a state, poor man, I thought he was going to cry." Michael put his head down. "His great-grandfather started that mill."

"How can they expect us to pay high bills right now?"

"It's the new government. Since they've taken over, the taxes have quadrupled. I'm scared we'll be in the same position. Not only that, but they told him he'd have to pay back taxes for the last three years. Can you believe that? Three years."

She looked around at her home. It was all she had left. Without it, there would be nothing. "How can they do this to us? We've suffered so much already."

"They want our property. They want everything."

"It's not fair." Her mind raced. "I have some family silver still buried under the house. Maybe I should start trying to find a buyer."

"No, don't do anything yet. You may need that to live on if worse comes to worst." He reached over and took her hand. "I'm glad you're here with me. You make these times bearable. Just knowing you're here, even though you won't marry me, makes me get through the day."

"You're still hurting an awful lot, aren't you?"

"It's not just a physical pain. It's an inward pain too. You'd think after all these months I'd be used to not having a leg, but it doesn't seem to get any better. I curse myself constantly for not being able to do what I want to do."

"I know it must be terrible, but you can't give up. We all need you. You're not helpless." She looked him straight in the eye. "I need you."

"But you don't love me."

Now Camille looked away from him. Her heart broke for not being able to give him what he needed. "I told you I love you, but it's just not the way you want me to."

Michael used his crutch to push himself up from the chair.

"Don't go, Michael. I want you to stay."

"No." He positioned the crutch. "I'm not good company tonight."

She stood up next to him. He leaned down, kissed her again, this time on the lips, a sweet kiss, gentle just like him. She smiled.

"I'm not giving up on you, Camille, you know that."

She nodded.

She'd give anything to love him as he wanted her to. He was kind and loving and would make a wonderful husband, but now she knew what it was like to have every inch of her being snap just standing near someone. She knew it was possible to have a person's memory warm her at night, even though he was miles away.

She had experienced all of this with Jake, and now she cursed him for it. He was gone forever, leaving her with a gaping void that probably would stay empty for a lifetime.

She watched Michael drive the buggy away before she went into the quiet house. Katherine had collapsed onto her bed as soon as they'd finished supper.

The typical July night was extremely warm so she selected a white gown, one of those that couldn't be salvaged from the mud stains of the road to New Orleans. Lifting it to her face, she placed her skin against the cool cotton. She touched the brown stains, remembering the road, the mud, and the man on the horse. She closed her eyes, but before going into worthless reveries, she pushed thoughts of Jake aside. She couldn't wallow in the past forever. The war might be over, but the struggle to survive had not ended.

She went through her nightly routine mechanically, shaking out her dress for tomorrow's rounds and then brushing her hair until it shone. Afterward she sat on the side of the bed and listened to the sounds of the night. There was something mysterious yet calming about what nature did in the dark. She closed her eyes and listened to a distant whip-poor-will.

When it stopped suddenly, she sat up straight, listened, then walked to the window and looked out. Nothing moved, but from down the road, the sound of a solitary horse broke the silence. She grabbed a robe, then lit a lantern.

From a window in the parlor, she caught a glimpse of a horse and rider as they turned into the unused carriage house. No one visited after dark since the war. It had to be news from her sister.

Without thinking of the danger, she darted out onto the porch and ran through the damp grass to the door of the carriage house. There, tending a huge horse, was a strange man with his back to her.

She stopped abruptly, her hands flying up to her mouth. She had expected someone familiar, like her uncle, but she could tell this man was not family. Shadows shielded his body from her view. She wanted to turn and run back to the house, but something about him froze her to her spot.

"Camille," he said as he faced her.

"Jake." Her heart raced. "Oh, God, Jake."

"Shh," he whispered. Stepping within inches of her, he took her in his arms and held her close. "Don't talk."

Her heart pounded with expectation, excitement, disbelief. He encircled her with his arms. After all the months of dreaming of him, pushing him out of her mind, and wanting him gone from her life, she melted into his embrace.

He lowered his head and crushed his lips to hers. A stab of ecstasy shot through her. There in the shadows of the carriage house, he held her and kissed her just as he had done in her dreams.

"I had no idea if you'd want me here," his breath was as jagged as hers. "But I couldn't leave without seeing you."

Camille stood before him unashamed that she had responded to his kisses. "Had you left without seeing me, I would've never forgiven you."

He ran his hand down the length of her hair. "Let's go inside."

Without hesitation, she took his hand and led him into the night. "Yes. I have a million questions, but first you must be starving."

"Not really, but I could use something to drink."

He followed her into the long kitchen running along the back of the house. She took a glass from the cupboard and pumped water. "It's all I have right now, but if you'd like, I could make some coffee.

"This is fine. Maybe before I leave, I'll take you up on that coffee so I won't fall asleep on the road."

She turned to face him. "You can't mean to leave. You just got here."

"I'll stay tonight, but I can't be here during the day. You'd be in more trouble with your community than you'd know how to handle. On second thought, maybe I'll stay and cause you enough trouble that you'll have to go with me."

She lowered her eyes. "Don't joke about a thing like that."

"I'm not joking, Millie."

She looked up and smiled. "Just to let you know, I'd probably hop on Moses and go with you."

He placed his hands on her arms. "I'd take you with me now, if I could, but I had a telegram waiting for me in New Orleans from my company saying that I have to report to Washington immediately. I thought I was heading home first, but I'm scheduled to appear before a house delegation or some nonsense that they want me involved in. Anyway, I have to get up there. I'm trying to resign my commission, but it may not be as easy as I thought."

"I'm so glad you came here, but it doesn't seem fair that I've got to lose you again so soon."

He sat and stretched his long legs. "I'm not sure how long I'll be away, but I promise I'll be back, that is, if you want me to."

She grabbed his hand. "Yes, I want you to come back."

In answer he pulled her down to him and kissed her sweetly on the forehead. She slid into him and put her arms around his neck. "I can't believe you're here. I've thought about you every day since you came to bring Charles home."

He nodded. "And I've never stopped thinking about you. I'm so sorry your mother died. It's not fair that she and Charles survived the war but never lived to see the beginning of what it will bring."

"Mother died peacefully. She just gave up, I think."

"Mr. Taloux told me that Dorothy moved from the coast, but Katherine stayed with you."

"Yes, Dorothy is helping on a farm about fifty miles from here, and Katherine is with me. Right now she's asleep. She's been a lifesaver to me and to the soldiers that we nurse."

"I'm glad you're not alone." He took a drink, then hesitated. "Uh, Mr. Taloux said the last time he saw you that you had a young man with you?"

Camille nodded. "Yes, my friend Michael came home last year missing a leg. I've been nursing him, and his family is helping me and my sister."

"Is that all?"

She smiled. "Why, Major Warren, are you questioning my social acquaintances?"

"Yes, as a matter of fact, I am. Is he just a family friend or is he a new beau?"

Camille stood up and refilled his glass. "He'd like to be more than a friend, but I can't reciprocate."

"Good."

"But I thought you just said you didn't want me to be alone."

"I did, but I was talking about a sister being with you, not some man."

"I wish I could see him as something more. Life would be much easier. Maybe I could've forgotten you and moved on with my life now that the war is over."

"But it's not easy, is it?"

"No, Jake, it's not, and you don't help the situation at all."

"I'm sorry. I didn't mean to complicate your life, but I can't say I'm sorry that you couldn't move on without me. It's what I've dreamed of."

"You really mean that?"

"You know I do, but, like I said, life isn't always easy."

He stood up and took her hand. "Let's go on the porch. I don't want to wake Katherine. I want you all to myself for a few hours."

In the dark of the front porch, Camille sat next to Jake on the swing. With his arm around her body, she placed her head on his shoulder. He smelled of Moses and perspiration from an all-day ride from the city, but it was a scent she'd remember always. Jake said he'd return, but Washington was a long way away, and she was afraid he'd realize how far removed their worlds were from each other once he returned to a normal life.

He stretched his long legs in front of him and relaxed against the back of the swing. Camille spoke of things that had happened since the war had ended, but before long she realized Jake was asleep.

From the light of the moon that had moved across the sky, she could see his eyelids twitch. Did he dream of the island prison or of his civilian life away from the ugliness of war?

The outline of his face was impressively strong with a firm chin and high cheekbones. Even in the dim light, she could see tiny lines around his eyes. Age lines? Stress lines? She had no idea how old he was, but knew that he was older and that the war had put as much stress on him as she had felt.

He was beautiful, like a dream that wasn't real. Her body ached for sleep, but she refused to close her eyes. Like a dream, he would be gone, and she wanted to remember every moment with him.

"You're staring." He startled her.

She laughed. "Did I wake you?"

"Yes," he said and pulled her close to him. "Thank you. I didn't come here to sleep. I just want to be with you."

"But you said you were leaving before daylight. You need a little sleep or Moses will drop you somewhere between here and New Orleans."

He chuckled. "Let's hope not. He knows who feeds him. He might drop me, but he won't leave me alone."

"That's a nice feeling to know you're not alone."

He faced her again. "And if things go as I want them to, I'll make sure you're never alone again."

Camille nodded, feeling the tear well behind her eyelids.

"You know I'll come back, don't you?" he asked as he worked his hand through her hair.

"I'll hold you to that, Major." She tried to smile, wanted to tell him that she loved him, but hesitated.

He pulled her close. Held her for a long moment, then whispered, "I love you, Millie. It's not fair to ask you to wait for me, but, God, how I want you to tell me you will."

"I want to wait for you, but how . . ." She looked up at him with tears in her eyes.

"How can we be together? Is that what you're asking?"

She nodded. "Your family. What will they think?"

"They won't like it, but they'll learn to accept it."

"I don't want to cause trouble for you. They've picked out your wife, it seems."

Jake chuckled. "They only think they did. Camille, I can't marry someone I don't love, and I love you. If you don't want to go to Rhode Island, we'll go elsewhere. The world is open to us. I just want us to be together."

Her tears refused to obey. They flooded her eyes and ran down her cheeks. "I'll wait for you. I couldn't do anything less. I love you."

"Then my ride here and back was worth it to hear you say those words. They'll get me through the rest of this duty."

For the rest of the night, they sat quietly, talking about a life together in a place where they'd be accepted for who they were, not from where they lived. They didn't know where that would be, but it didn't matter. One day, they'd have the wonderful problem of figuring that part out.

For now, Camille was content to hear his words of love and hope they stayed with him when he left.

The first streak of pink in the eastern sky told them their time together was over. He followed her into the house and drank a quick cup of coffee. After placing his cup in the dishpan, he picked up a small carved fish that lay by the fireplace. "What this?"

Camille smiled. "It's my lucky charm, my magical dream catcher. My papa carved it for me when I was very small. We didn't have a lot. He was a doctor and material things weren't important to him. He said if I had this magical fish by my side, I could have anything in the world that I wanted."

She reached out and rubbed her fingers over the carving. "These are wings. He said a fish with wings had the best of both worlds. He could take me places no one else could ever go. Of course, it took me a while to figure out that these places were only in my mind."

"So you've gone places alone all these years with the help of your magical fish."

She nodded. "I know it's silly, but it's kept me company many lonely nights, especially during the war. I could close my eyes and imagine wonderful things."

Jake pulled her close to him. "Well, you keep this

little fish by you and when you climb into bed by
yourself, close your eyes and dream of me."

"I don't need a magical charm to do that."

Camille leaned against the door of the carriage
house and watched Jake saddle Moses. When he was
satisfied that it was right, he pulled Camille into his
arms one last time.

"I can't bear to see you go," she whispered.

"I know, but I swear, I'll be back." He kissed her
long and hard, then jumped on Moses' back and left
abruptly.

Camille watched him gallop down the shell road.
She longed to run after him, throw common sense to
the wind, and make him take her along. She had survived a war. She could take care of herself in Washington or wherever he was sent.

But her life was here, at least for the moment, and
she would continue to live it until Jake Warren returned. Far down the road, Jake raised his arm and
turned in a final farewell gesture. Then he was gone.

Chapter Twelve

August 1865

It had been like a dream.

At times she wondered if she had imagined Jake coming to her in the middle of the night, but then she only had to close her eyes to know it had been real. Those thoughts sustained her for the days and weeks that followed his leaving.

One day, returning home from her rounds, she opened the gate as a well-dressed man stopped his carriage on the road. He tipped his hat to her. "Good day, ma'am. Would you happen to know where the Hollander home is?"

Her heart pounded against her chest. This stranger could only mean bad news. Jake, taxes, something. She found her voice. "I'm Miss Hollander. How can I help you?"

He reached out a plump hand. She reciprocated with a shake as weak as his own.

"My name is Mr. Schmidt, Mr. Earnest Schmidt, with the tax collection office for this district. Is your mother home?"

Camille breathed a sigh of relief that he wasn't the bearer of bad news from her family or from Jake. She knew about taxes. She could handle this, even though she didn't want to.

"My mother died recently. I'll be glad to talk with you if you'll come up on the porch."

She watched him struggle down from the carriage. When he reached the porch he plopped down in one of their rockers and took a deep breath.

"What can I do for you?"

He cleared his throat. "I'm personally going around to the homes of you nice people delivering your new property assessments. I'm here at your service. I'd like you to look over the papers and ask me any questions before I leave."

He handed her a large envelope, never mentioning the death of her mother. She ripped it open with no expression on her face, but when she saw the figures on the paper, she went white. "Who did the assessments?"

"The government did. I'm here on their behalf. Uh, we're giving our citizens one month to come up with the money. If there're no other questions, I'll leave you. Oh, by the way, here's my card. I'm also in real estate so if you can't come up with the money for the taxes, I might be interested in purchasing the house. At least you'll have some money in your pocket in the end. There seems to be a shortage of buyers in these parts."

His smile was almost wicked. With a nod, he turned to go. "Keep us in mind, Miss Hollander. You'll be happy I came by today."

Camille sat, numb. It was just as Michael had said. Taxes had quadrupled, not to count the three years of back taxes that would also have to be paid. For a long moment she allowed herself to wallow in self-pity. Maybe she should've ridden off with Jake and started a life somewhere up north. Forget about the house. Forget about what her papa had built with his bare hands.

Starting a life with Jake would be wonderful, but was she ready to leave her home right now?

She stood up and threw down the envelope. She and her neighbors had lost a lot during the war, but they had managed to hold onto their property and their dignity. Now she wasn't so sure they could still hold their heads up.

Her mind reeled. There had to be a way to beat this, to pay the taxes and keep her family home, but the more she thought, the more despondent she became. Money was almost nonexistent. Ten families together couldn't come up enough to pay these taxes.

She picked up the envelope and wiped it off. There's bound to be a way. *They can't break us!*

But in her heart she knew that probably she and the other locals would have to concede, just as their generals had done.

The next morning another carriage pulled up to her gate. Camille took a deep breath before opening the curtain, then broke into a big smile. It was her sister Dorothy.

Camille ran out the front door and the two sisters hugged at the gate.

"Let me look at you, Dorothy," Camille said as she held her at arm's length. "You look wonderful. You don't know how good it is to see you." Dorothy wore a day dress of soft yellow cotton. The fabric wasn't new and Camille assumed it was a hand-me-down from someone around the small community where she lived. She was thrilled for her sister.

"You look good too, Camille." Dorothy looked around at the man who had driven up with her. "I want you to meet someone. This is Paul Jackson, my fiancé."

"Camille. I've heard a lot about you." He reached out his hand.

Camille's mouth fell open. "Oh, my word, this is wonderful." She started to shake his hand, changed her mind, and hugged him instead. "My baby sister's getting married. I can't believe it."

"Where's Katherine? I want to share my news with her."

"She's down the road. She'll be home soon. Come in. There's so much to catch up on."

The three of them sat around the kitchen table waiting for Katherine. Dorothy explained that she and Paul would be married the following week in his local church near Wiggins.

"Please tell me you and Katherine can come up. It'll be small, but Aunt Betsy is baking a cake and several of the neighbors will bring over treats of some sort. Mr. McNally said he'd bring in his harmonica and we'd have a little dance. I can't get married without my sisters with me."

Camille knew with so much happening, she shouldn't leave, but this was her sister. "We'll be there. Michael has a buggy and a horse, so maybe he can take a day or so off and ride up with us."

That night the three sisters sat alone and Camille explained about the taxes, trying to prepare Dorothy for the inevitable. Dorothy shed tears and begged Camille to do something to save the only home that they had ever known.

By the time Dorothy and Paul rode off the next morning, Camille felt worse than ever. Paul had cursed the Yankees for what they were doing. He carried around a huge scar on his shoulder where a bullet went clear through him, so he was unrelenting when it came to anyone who fought for the north.

Tears stung Camille's eyes when she finally went inside, not just from the taxes, but the situation she found herself in. She didn't know what to scream about first, the fact that she would lose her family home or the fact that Jake would never be accepted here, ever, no matter how good a man he was or how much she loved him.

And that was a fact. She did love him, and that in itself would have to get her through the bad times that were coming.

The next afternoon after coming in from looking after four men on the other side of the bay, Camille stripped the linens from the bed to wash, then carried the pillows out on the porch to air.

After throwing the pillows on the swing, she turned to see another carriage coming down the road. She stopped suddenly. "Now what?"

She tried to think positive by fluffing the pillows as she watched the man drive up and stop at her gate. She groaned.

A stout, rugged-looking man stepped out of the carriage. "Hello to you," he greeted her from the road. Camille didn't recognize him or what he wore. His black pants and silky shirt under a black, gold-trimmed coat was definitely not like any uniform she'd ever seen.

He opened the gate. "I'm looking for a Miss Camille Hollander. Could that be you, Miss?"

Camille nodded. "Yes, sir." Frantically, her mind flew from one event in her life to the next trying to place this individual and why he could possibly be asking for her.

He stuck a big cigar in his mouth, lit it, then after a few puffs took it out and addressed her. "I beg your pardon for just dropping in on you like this, but I have a package for you. I've talked to every inhabitant along these shores trying to find this house. I've never been down so many shell roads in my life." He stepped back to the carriage and lifted a large package from the back bench. Another larger one sat next to it.

After placing the package on the porch, he fumbled around the pockets of his coat and pulled out an envelope.

Camille stood unmoving. She had never received a package before, and she wasn't sure what she was supposed to do. In her lifetime she had only received one personal letter and that was from a cousin.

"Let me introduce myself," the large man finally said through the side of his mouth, the cigar still hanging from his teeth. My name is Admiral Vernon Buckley. My ship is the *Maritime*. Right now I'm anchored off shore. My mission today is to deliver this package to you. It's from Major Warren. He asked me personally to get it to you."

"Major Warren sent this to me?" Her breath caught in her throat and tears stung her eyes.

The admiral handed her the letter. She rubbed her

thumb over it in awe, then remembered her manners. "Can I offer you a glass of water?"

"Yes, that'd be nice, and I'll get the other package while you're inside."

Camille nearly knocked over a chair hurrying to the kitchen for his water, and was back out on the porch before he returned with the large package. Together, they sat, he in a rocker, she in the swing. Very carefully she unfastened the seal on the back of the envelope and pulled out a beautifully written letter and another smaller envelope.

Dear Camille,

There is so much I want to say, but because of discretion, I cannot in this letter. Our recent meeting has sustained me and renewed my soul, but it will not last forever. I must see you again. My orders are for the Washington area, but they are temporary, several months at the most, I hope. After a visit to RI, I will finish my business in Washington, then I plan to travel to Mississippi before my next orders.

The packages are for you. Please don't look at them as charity. I know you want to start a small business for yourself and your sisters. These items would be difficult for you to find. The money is for taxes since I know how outrageous they have become. Please accept everything as a gesture from my heart. It is all I can give right now. I will see you as soon as humanly possible. The future awaits us.

Sincerely, Jake.

Camille sat for several minutes staring at the signature, then opened the smaller envelope to find federal bills. In disbelief, she counted more than enough to pay the taxes on her home. No way could she hold back the tears that spilled down her cheeks.

Admiral Buckley shuffled his feet, getting her attention. "Jake has been my friend for many years, and during our voyage to Washington, I could tell he thinks a great deal of you. He is a man of few words, at least to me, but it wasn't hard to read what he was feeling."

Camille wiped her tears away with her bare hand. "Thank you so much. You can't image how much this means to me. Will you see him again?"

"Yes, the ship'll make a quick stop in Washington in a couple of weeks. I'll look him up if you'd like to send something to him. A letter perhaps." He looked at his pocket watch. "I don't have much time before I have to get back to my ship, but I'll wait if you'll be quick about it. I'll open the boxes for you so you can thank him properly."

Camille flew inside and found only one small piece of paper that could be used for a correspondence. Paper was scarce and had been used up early in the war. Quickly she penned a reply, discreet, but caring. He would know how she felt. As a last thought, she grabbed the small, carved fish, caressing it gently, the way she knew he would do.

"Make sure he gets this along with the letter. He'll understand."

Admiral Buckley waved good-bye from the buggy, with her short note and small carving tucked safely in his inside pocket. She had to use Jake's envelope for her reply, but she knew he would understand.

Dorothy's morning wedding was simple but beautiful. She wore a pale blue dress that had belonged to Paul's mother and carried wild flowers as she vowed to live with Paul forever. Staying only long enough to taste a small cake that was put together from neighborhood donations, Michael, Camille, and Katherine headed home.

Michael flicked the reins as the buggy neared the coast. "Dorothy looked beautiful, didn't she?"

Camille nodded. She'd been in deep thought since their departure and had said very little to Michael or Katherine who sat on the back bench.

"Are you sad that she's married?" he asked.

"Oh, no, what makes you say such a thing? I'm thrilled for her."

"You haven't said a word since we left from up there."

She placed a hand on his. "I'm sorry, Michael. My

mind is just a million miles away right now." *Washington, to be exact.*

"When are they coming down?"

Camille forced her attention to their conversation. "Paul said maybe next week so he can help you and your father with the shop. That would give them time to get their things together."

"You won't mind them living with you?"

"It'll be different, but the house is big. We'll manage."

"You know my offer still stands," he said hopefully. "You could always come move in with us."

"I know. And that's very kind of you, but I wouldn't feel right. I'm happy where I am."

"You shouldn't be alone, Camille." He acted as if he wanted to say more but he didn't.

Guilt made Camille avert her eyes. He loved her. She loved Jake.

Jake's money paid the taxes on her house and helped finish the taxes on the Rice home. In repayment, Mr. Rice donated the wood for her business and helped her build the shop. She wasn't sure if she would be around to actually run the shop, but it could be used to support her sisters and now Paul.

In the back of her mind she kept thinking that one day Jake could be part of the business also, but deep in her heart she knew that probably wouldn't be possible.

She had also told Michael he could be part of it if it ever got to the point that working in the mill was too much for him. She doubted that would ever come about either.

She awoke to the sound of saws in her backyard. Michael and Mr. Rice were cutting lumber to begin boarding up around the frame that some of the men in the village helped them raise. It was a good sound, a sound of rebuilding, and she felt good to be a part of it.

When she brought out a bowl of potato soup for their lunch and coffee made from boiled peanuts, Mr. Rice sat next to her.

"Camille, I've been meaning to talk to you about something."

She looked up.

"Uh, I don't know how to tell you this, and don't take this as just my opinion, but there's been a lot of talk among the menfolk that you shouldn't be doing this business thing."

Her brows came together. "What do you mean?"

"Like I said, they think a woman shouldn't own her own business, at least this kind of business. A dress shop maybe, but not a shop for men who fish. It's just not ladylike."

"But it's my property and my idea, and no one else is going to take care of me and mine." Her voice rose with each word. "It was okay for me to work like a man as long as the war was going on, but now that it's over, I'm supposed to become a helpless lady again, is that it?"

"You don't understand. You're not even supposed to own property. This is your pa's property. Not yours. This building can't even be yours."

Camille slammed down her bowl of soup, spilling it onto the porch. "You can't be serious. It's my building and my business. If I have to put my father's name on it even though he's dead, so be it, but it's mine."

"People around here won't agree. I was preparing you for what's to come. You can't use your father's name. He's dead. I suggest you put Paul's name on the deed. Like that, it stays in the family and everyone's happy."

"No, sir, not everyone. I've worked too hard these last three years to be treated like a brainless fool."

"No one thinks you're a brainless fool. They only want you to be a lady again, and a lady doesn't start her own fishing business."

"I'm tired of people telling me what a lady can do. I could start a sewing business, but that's not where the money will be. I know in my heart that this place on the water will make money for my family. It's my idea. My business. My name."

Mr. Rice let out a long breath. "It might be your idea, but the building will have to be in a man's name."

She stood up. "All of you are impossible." Taking her bowl of half-spilled soup, she marched inside fighting back tears of frustration.

Michael followed. "Camille, I know how you must feel."

She spun around. "Do you, Michael? I've supported my family throughout this war just like most of the women around here. I've fished, nursed, dried salt. I'm not going to let this town treat me this way."

He balanced himself on his crutch and put a hand on her arm. "You can't fight the government. That's the way it is. It doesn't matter whose name is on the deed. Everyone will know it's yours."

"It doesn't matter whose name is on the deed as long as it's not my name," she answered sarcastically.

He sighed. "Yes."

"We'll see about that."

"I give up. You're the most aggravating female I've ever run into."

That made her laugh. "Well, then, stay out of my way, and I won't run into you."

At that they both laughed. He took her hand, but the smile still plastered on his face couldn't hide the sadness in his eyes. "You're quite a woman, Camille. You do what you have to do. Just remember that I'm here for you if you need me."

"Michael, I . . ."

"Don't say anything. You know, I've latched onto you since I got back, and I've ruined it between us."

"No, no, don't ever say that."

"Would you listen? Like I was saying, I've latched onto you because I truly do love you, but it could never work for us. I know that now, and I guess I knew it all along. I was just dreaming for something that could never be. You'll always be my friend, and I'll always love you for that."

Camille stood motionless, unable to bring up the words of relief she felt.

The next morning she marched down the road to the small building where the government had set up office. She'd made her mind up before she got there. She couldn't have her name on the property, but no one said she couldn't put Jake's.

"You did what?" Paul spun around with the last armload of possessions that he and Dorothy were moving into the house. Dorothy stepped away from him, her eyes huge. "You put a Yankee's name of your father's land. You expect me to work something that belongs to him?"

"No, Paul, it doesn't belong to him. He doesn't even know his name is on the deed, but you know what? Rightfully he has more claim to it than any of us do. It was his money that saved the land and his money that provided this lumber from the Rice mill. Without it, there wouldn't even be a mill."

Paul yanked up the last load of bedding and marched into Dorothy's old bedroom. Dorothy backed against the hall wall.

"I guess you're upset too?" Camille spit her words out.

"I don't know what to say. I don't approve of all this, especially with your putting that man's name on our land."

Camille reeled in her temper and tried to speak in a calm voice. "Dorothy, you begged me to save your home. It's done. Now live with it. We have a home, but if we don't find some way to make money over the next year, there won't be a home when tax time comes around again."

"But it's Yankee money."

"Yes, but without it, this house would be a Yankee house."

"It already is with—" She hesitated, as if saying his name was a blasphemy.

"With Jake's name on the deed? You can say it, Dorothy. He gave us the money as a gift. Take it for what it is."

Paul stepped out of the bedroom. "And what will he do with the property when he finds out he owns it?"

Camille started to defend Jake, but decided not to. Paul would never understand. Instead she turned to Dorothy.

"I suggest if you and Paul want someplace to live, you pitch in and help make this business work."

Camille spun around. How would she ever convince her family that the man they thought responsible for her brother's death was someone who had given her reason to live?

Chapter Thirteen

September 1865

The completed tackle shop, stocked with the items from Jake, sat empty for over a week waiting for its first customer. Camille locked the door and tacked a note to it, explaining where she could be found if anyone showed up.

Her community had turned against her just because of a name on a piece of paper, but she refused to let them take away the hope that Jake would return for her.

Paul met her as she walked across the lawn back to the house. "I told you this would never work. That man ruined everything. Everyone knows you've switched sides."

Camille swallowed the hurt. "I didn't switch sides. The war is over. One day these people will understand."

"Understand what? That my sister-in-law turned her back on her family?"

She spun around and faced him. "I did what had to be done. You know everything here and down the road at the Rice home is still ours because of Jake. You're blind to what he did for us."

"And you're blind thinking people will forget."

Paul left her standing in the middle of the yard, but turned around and yelled, "I'm taking Dorothy back home. At least there we have dirt that will grow enough to live on."

Camille didn't answer. If that's what he needed to do, then she wouldn't stand in his way. She hadn't heard from Jake since Admiral Buckley had delivered the package, but she had to believe he hadn't forgotten her. She didn't expect Paul or anyone else to understand. It would take time to go to Rhode Island and then back down to Washington. She had no idea how long, but she knew she had to be patient.

By the end of the next week, a young boy rode up to her door with a telegram. Her heart pounded as she read:

WILL BE IN WASHINGTON FOR SOME TIME. PLEASE COME MEET ME. A TRAIN RUNS FROM MOBILE. SEND WORD OF TIME OF ARRIVAL IN CARE OF THE WEST-BURY HOUSE. DON'T DELAY. I'LL BE

WAITING WITH A MINISTER TO MARRY
US IF YOU'LL AGREE. LOVE, JAKE.

Camille closed her eyes and held the telegram close
to her heart. He was waiting for her, and there was no
reason for her to delay. Her life had been put in order
here. The business and house would be taken over by
Dorothy and Paul. They had threatened to leave, but as
soon as she was no longer here, she was sure customers would come into the shop.

She shook her head. It was unbelievable to her
how she'd been shunned.

By nightfall she'd put a plan of action into place.
For hours she lay awake. Her body needed the rest, but
her mind raced from thought to thought. This night
could be the last she'd ever spend in this house. Her
gaze took in everything in her room that had been part
of her life, each reminiscent of a time when she was so
different.

It was hard to imagine not being part of this fishing town and its people, and a feeling of sheer panic
swept over her as she thought about what the next
day had in store for her. Leon, one of the Darcey
workmen, would pick her up at daybreak and she'd
begin her journey to meet the man she loved.

Would she be accepted in Washington? Would his
family take her in, or would Jake be shunned as she
had been? Would he hold it against her if they did?

Question upon question raced through her mind, but even with them all unanswered, there was no doubt about what she wanted to do.

Shortly before daylight with only a couple hours of rest, she sat on the porch waiting for her carriage. She wore a crisp blue traveling suit and hat, given to her by Mrs. Darcey. Even though she had a little of Jake's money left, there was no fabric on the coastline to purchase.

She ran her hand down the cool fabric. One day she'd repay the Darceys for all they'd done for her. Even knowing they supported her now because of their friendship with Jake, she still admired them for being so kind and warm.

She'd wanted to look her best for Jake when she arrived, and Mrs. Darcey didn't hesitate to offer an outfit. She hoped the carriage ride wouldn't ruin it, but hours later when they pulled in front of her boardinghouse in Mobile, Camille almost cried at the dust that covered her clothes.

Leon helped her down from the carriage. She immediately brushed her skirt with her hand.

"Ma'am, I'm afraid it's not going to help. That train is almost as bad as this here open carriage, or at least that's what I come to hear about them."

"Oh, Leon, I'm so upset. I've never owned anything as nice as this. I should've known better than to wear it."

He hauled down two big bags. "I wouldn't worry

about no dust, ma'am. That man of yours won't care what you look like when you arrive. He's just waitin' to see you." He carried her bags into the boarding-house and made sure she was settled before saying his good-byes.

After washing off quickly, she took out her parasol and walked briskly to the train station. There, she found out the time of departure and bought a ticket as far as the Atlanta station.

Feeling good about her schedule so far, she planned to relax a bit with a walk and take in the sights in Mobile, but as soon as she stepped out the door of the train station, a man stepped in her path.

"Good day, little lady. What a coincidence meetin' you here in Mobile." He grinned and stuck a big cigar into his mouth. "Let me introduce myself. I'm Captain Bartholomew Avery."

Camille's vision blurred. This was the man who'd stabbed Jake. How did he know who she was? Had he been following her? Spying on her at her home?

Her head spun, but she refused to show weakness in front of this man. She grabbed the door for balance and stood her ground. People jammed the train station so she knew that at the moment she was safe.

Avery looked exactly as Jake had described him, even to his odor. Even though he wore a coat of gaudy pink brocade, it looked expensive and well made.

A jagged scar on the side of his face cut deep into

his skin, the scar that Jake said he'd given him. Deep purple in spots, it pulled the skin around his eye and distorted the entire side of his face. She shuddered.

"I see that the cat must have your tongue." His words slurred from the thick cigar he swirled around his mouth. "I guess not having any of your neighbors to talk to has gotten you in the habit of being silent. That's an admirable quality I like in my womenfolk."

"Sir, I don't know you. If you'll excuse me, I'm in a hurry. Someone's waiting for me, and I'm late," she lied. At that she pushed past him and out into the street. She dared not look over her shoulder to see if he followed her. No way would she give him the satisfaction of knowing he had shattered her peace of mind.

When she crossed the street, she looked from the corner of her eye, surprised not to see him. Stopping, she strained to see into the station through the cloudy windowpanes. Even from across the street, she thought she spotted Avery's pink coat at the ticket booth.

Ignoring the tightness in her chest, she hurried into her boardinghouse to await the departure of her train the next morning. The lovely homes and shops that had caught her attention on her way into the city would have to wait for another visit. She dared not leave the safety of the boardinghouse with Avery in town.

After dinner in a private dining room, she returned to her room and sat by the window, wondering if Avery knew where she was staying or where she was going. Could he be following her to get to Jake?

Should she go to the police? What would she report? The man had not threatened her today.

She longed to talk to Jake.

Finally, well after midnight she fell into a light, fitful sleep, only to wake up before daylight. Quietly, she prepared for the next leg of her trip. With the help of a hackney, she loaded her bags on the train and selected a seat near the back of a car.

She scrutinized each passenger who entered the car, fearful that any one of them could be Avery, but finally the whistle blew and the conductor shouted out his warning.

The train rumbled and vibrated and for the first time since she had seen Avery, she breathed a sigh of relief, but only for a second. The vibrations shook the car so violently she was sure the train would explode. She held onto her seat and waited to see if the other passengers would run out. When they didn't, she tried to relax.

Well into the night, the conductor came through and announced that there would be a rather long layover in Montgomery for the train to take on more water and coal.

Camille brushed the sleep from her eyes and stretched, then followed the others off the car to the back of the depot to use the outside facilities. It was humiliating having to wait in line when everyone knew what you were waiting to do, but she had no choice. Other passengers didn't seem to mind.

She gritted her teeth and waited her turn. Later she went into the dimly lit depot where coffee was being served.

"Tiring trip, isn't it?" someone said from behind her.

Camille stiffened. Just from the scent of the cologne, she knew Captain Avery stood near her. The man's slow, muddled words took her breath away. She closed her eyes.

Quickly regaining her composure, she turned and smiled at him. "It's not all that bad. In fact, we're enjoying it greatly."

"We're?" he asked with a devilish grin. "I could've sworn you were traveling alone. I haven't seen anyone with you. Of course, now, ole Captain's eyes aren't what they used to be"—he rubbed his hand across his scar—"but, you know, I'm really not blind yet."

"You'll just have to look harder next time, I guess." She turned, but he kept talking.

"You're on your way to Atlanta, huh?"

Camille ignored him.

"Well, I just figured maybe that's where that major was living now. I got word that he'd been around to see you."

Camille couldn't hide her annoyance. "How dare you spy on my private life! It's no business of yours who visits my home."

Avery shrugged. "I hear it's not even your home anymore. You see, I just can't keep my men from seeing and telling what they see, and it's a well-known fact around the bayou that he was around. Of course, by the time it got to me in Mobile, he'd already skedaddled."

He took a deep breath and rubbed his shoulder. "Wasn't hard to put two and two together when my men told me you got that telegram yesterday. I said to myself that the major lived somewhere up on the Atlanta side of the world. This here train goes to Atlanta, then another one connects with it and then runs to Washington and one runs somewhere around Virginia. I figured that any of those three places would be good for him to be working."

Camille fumed, but said nothing.

"How am I doing? Close? I figured the simplest way to find out was just to let you take me to him. We have business to finish."

Camille had turned her back to him while she waited in line for her coffee. Avery didn't give up. He rambled on. She thought she was doing a good job of appearing unmoved by him, but when she reached for her coffee, her hand shook violently, spilling the coffee onto the floor.

"Oh, yeah, I figure you're going to meet the major," Avery continued, "somewhere around Atlanta. I'm sure glad he came to see you. I'd love to even up the score with him for locking me in that dungeon, not to mention this blasted scar."

From the corner of her eye, Camille watched him rub his big hand across his face again. She shuddered.

"Yes, little lady, you made my searching easy."

Without acknowledging him again, she placed her cup on a table and walked away. She mingled with some of the other passengers, trying to appear calm, trying to keep the tears at bay. When she glanced at him over her shoulder, he tipped his hat overdramatically and made his exit to his train car. She collapsed in a seat.

What was she going to do? She couldn't lead Avery to Jake. If she warned him by telegraph here, Avery might be able to find out where it was going, find him and kill him. Right now, all Avery knew was that she was going to Atlanta. He didn't know she was going to Washington, and Camille wasn't about to lead him there.

There wasn't much of a decision to make.

When she was sure that Avery would stay in his car, she hurried to the ticket counter, bought a ticket back to Mobile, and requested that her bags be removed with as little attention as possible.

In a dark corner of the waiting room, she sat alone. Her train would not arrive until noon the next day, so she made herself comfortable. She would find the telegraph office in the morning to wire Jake.

With that thought, a sadness engulfed her. She'd been on her way to begin a life with Jake, and now, again, she would have to wait. In fact, at this point, with Avery back in the picture, her life with Jake could be only a dream that might never be lived.

The carriage and driver that Camille had hired rolled along the Spanish Trail. On her way to Mobile to catch the train, she'd taken in all the sights, studied each carriage they met, talked with Leon about her excitement. Now three days after beginning her journey, she sat in a daze, not seeing anyone or anything. Tired and dirty, she felt as empty and lonely as she had never had before in her life.

Assuming that Dorothy's husband, Paul, would rant and rave about "that Union officer" putting them all in danger, she directed the driver to the Darcey home. In her state of mind, she was afraid she'd cause discontent between Dorothy and her new husband.

When the carriage pulled through the tall gates, Camille looked down at herself. She tried to knock off the dust from her new outfit and pushed aside strands of hair that hung around her face. It was hopeless. Giving up, she walked up to the big front door, but Mrs. Darcey opened it before Camille could knock.

"I thought I heard a carriage pull up. What happened?" She reached out and took Camille's hand, but looked over her shoulder at the carriage.

"Mrs. Darcey, I hate to barge in like this. I have a little bit of a problem. Can I talk with you?"

"Why certainly, dear. Tell your coachman to go around back to freshen up."

This being done, Camille followed the lady into the parlor. It hadn't changed a bit from the horrible day she remembered seeing Jake socializing with Mrs. Darcey's friends. Unconsciously, she looked at where he had stood.

"Sit. Alice will bring you a drink. Now tell me what happened." Sitting next to her, the older woman reached out and took Camille's hand again.

"I didn't know where else to go." Camille explained everything, even going back to the time that Avery had been in Jake's prison and his attack on him. Mrs. Darcey sat wide-eyed through it all, sipping her tea delicately, but riveting her gaze on Camille as she talked.

"Oh, my," Mrs. Darcey said when Camille finally finished. "This is really exciting. I mean, it's horrible, but it's exciting also. Oh, I'm so pleased that you came to me."

She got up and paced up and down in front of Camille. "We must first send a telegram to let Major Warren know you're with us and safe. I'm sure he must be beside himself."

"Thank you, ma'am. I didn't take the time to send a message to him before leaving. I was so afraid Avery would see me. I knew I could count on you."

"I wouldn't have it any other way. You don't worry, now. I'll get everything straightened. You two must be together. Now, you stay here and I'll get Joseph to bring your bags in."

"Uh, I was going to ask if I could rent the guest-house from you. Like that, if I'm stuck here for sometime, I won't feel as if I'm imposing on your family."

"Nonsense. You'll stay right here in this house. We have several spare bedrooms. I wouldn't think of letting you sleep out there alone with that man Avery on the loose. We'll have Alice air one of the rooms for you."

"Thank you," Camille answered and sincerely meant it. A heavy burden slipped from her shoulders. Michael's family would have taken her in, but she wouldn't have felt comfortable under the circumstances, and her sisters had already made it clear that they didn't approve of Jake. Here, she felt wanted and not regarded as a traitor.

That night as she lay in the big featherbed, she ached to have Jake beside her as her husband. As long as she kept her eyes closed, she could pretend Jake was there. The second she opened them, there was nothing but the humid night air settling in around her and the lingering remembrance of Avery's cologne.

Had it not been for that wretched man, she would have been Mrs. Jake Warren by nightfall.

She swung her legs over the side of the bed and sat motionless in the semidarkness of the room, trying to rid herself of the gripping ache in her heart. She tried to plan her next course of action. Already, Mrs.

Darcey had wired Jake that she would stay with them until he wired her back with instructions. She hoped—she prayed—that it would not be long until he replied.

She poured a small amount of water into a bowl. It was lukewarm, but splashing a little on her face refreshed her somewhat. From the second-story window, she could look out over the bay to the south where she had traveled to meet Jake or look to the north at the shore where she'd spent her life.

A yearning tugged at her heart. This had been her home, her life, and now she was leaving it forever. Already feeling like a stranger there, she sighed and crawled back under the light coverlet. With Jake lying next to her in her mind, she let the exhaustion from the trip overcome her. Within minutes, she was asleep.

The next day started early for Camille, and during most of it, she found herself sitting on the porch or walking near the bay waters waiting for a telegram. She could see her little shop in the distance if she stood near the water's edge, but she had no desire to go over to check on it. She knew that Dorothy would have it under control; in fact, her presence alone would probably hurt business. The way the community had ostracized her for accepting Jake's help made her wonder if she could ever be, or ever want to be, part of it again.

Her concern now was for her life with Jake and

staying clear of Avery. She broke a twig and threw it into the water. Why hadn't she received a telegram? Surely Jake had gotten hers by now. Twenty-four hours was plenty enough time to reply.

She refused to think of reasons why he had not.

Mrs. Darcey and her husband walked up behind her. She wore a light cotton dress and bonnet in pale yellow, making her look fresh and younger than her real age. Mr. Darcey looked healthier than he had in years.

"Don't look so sad. You'll receive word soon." Mrs. Darcey's eyes lit up. "You know what I'm going to do? Joseph!" she called, before revealing her plan to Camille. "We'll send him across the bay to see if they've received a telegram. Sometimes those men in the telegraph office can't get over here right away."

Camille threw her arms around Mrs. Darcey. "Thank you so much."

For the rest of the afternoon, Camille paced up and down the porch or walked the water's edge waiting for Joseph's return.

"Camille, you've got to relax, darling. You're going to make yourself ill worrying like this. Joseph had some other errands to run while he was over in Biloxi so it might be a little while before he gets back, but I'm sure he won't be much longer."

"I know, ma'am. I guess I'm being silly."

"Oh, no, you're not being silly at all. This Captain Avery business is very serious. I'd be upset also."

They walked together under the low-hanging branches of a big oak tree, then continued to the pier.

Mrs. Darcey touched her arm and pointed to the big channel where Camille spotted Joseph's boat. Tears welled in her eyes.

As the boat neared, Joseph waved his hand frantically. "Got your message, Miss Camille. Got it right here."

"Oh, I knew my prayers would be answered," Camille said to herself.

Joseph took only a moment to pull the boat up to the pier and to climb up with Camille's assistance.

Camille took the telegram from him. Her heart pounded.

YOU'RE IN GOOD HANDS. STAY THERE. DO NOT COME MEET ME OR LEAVE TOWN. I LOVE YOU. JAKE.

Mrs. Darcey put her arms on Camille's shoulders. "I'm so glad he got your message. He didn't say it, but I'll just bet he'll find his way here."

Camille nodded and didn't try to hide the tears of joy that ran down her cheeks.

Not knowing were Jake was, where Avery was, or what would happen next, Camille watched the days creep into one week, then into two. Mr. Darcey advised her not to leave the house since Avery's men could find out where she was staying, even though she assumed her arrival was public news by now.

News traveled fast between the small towns, so for her own safety, she stayed near the house helping Mrs. Darcey with her sewing and cooking, and even playing checkers with Mr. Darcey.

At the beginning of the third week of her stay, Camille wet the hook of a cane pole as she sat with Alice on the pier. With the young girl babbling on about her young man that she was about to marry and the sun warming her back, Camille fished quietly and let the afternoon pass. For the moment she even forgot Jake was somewhere without her and Avery was threatening her peace.

The outline of her shop was barely visible in the distance, but she knew exactly what it looked like and in her mind she could see every detail. She wondered if the customers forgave Dorothy for having a sister who was running off with a Yankee.

As she looked from the shop out toward the bay opening, she saw a boat heading in their direction. Camille squinted to make out its lines. It was too far away to make out any details, but she could tell that it was definitely coming their way.

"Alice, do you recognize that boat?"

Alice shaded her eyes and strained to see. "No, ma'am, I don't know that boat. Just some fisherman probably."

Camille agreed, but watched it closely. Her chest tightened.

"I think I'll go in now. I'm terribly hot in this sun," she said, then rose and put her pole down.

"Yes, ma'am, you ought to have your parasol or at least a sun bonnet. This sun can sure enough put freckles on your nose."

Both girls laughed, each knowing that was Camille's last concern.

Camille turned to leave and took one last look at the boat. Only two men were in it, and it was traveling very close to the shoreline, much too close to be going into the bayou. It seemed to be heading right toward the pier.

Turning quickly, she hurried toward the house.

"Miss Camille! Miss Camille!" shouted Alice. "That man's waving his hand like he wants you."

Camille's breath came in gulps. Almost too terrified to turn around, she knew it could be Avery sitting in the boat, loving the fact that Camille was running from him. She gritted her teeth, clenched her fists, and turned.

The bright sunshine and the glare from the water made it difficult to see clearly. She had to squint to actually see the boat.

"Camille!" came a familiar voice from the boat. "Camille, it's me." Jake jumped out of the boat and onto the pier even before it had stopped. He ran down the planks toward Camille.

Camille stood unmoving until the realization of the moment struck her. Jake had come for her.

She grabbed the bottom of her skirt and ran, meeting him with outstretched arms. He lifted her up off the ground, crushing her body to his. He kissed her on the face and hair and mouth. Finally he relaxed his hold and put her down.

"My God, Camille, you're safe. I was afraid Avery would beat me back here when he realized you had slipped away from him."

"I'm safe now. You came. I've been so afraid, but it was for you. I was sure he'd figure out where you were."

"He didn't." At that he pulled her to him and held her head against his chest. His heart pounded in her ears and she clung to him as if her life depended on it.

"I hate to break up this little reunion, but it's hot standing here in the sun."

Camille looked up to see the other man from the boat standing next to them.

Jake kept his arm around Camille. "Vernon, sorry to ignore you."

"Captain Buckley, you brought him home for me." Camille opened one arm to him and he too embraced her.

That night Camille and Jake sat alone in the parlor of the big house, her head resting on his shoulder as he cuddled her close. Tomorrow they would be married

by the local priest, but for now they sat in quiet antici-
pation of tomorrow night.

For three weeks each had lived in a state of not
knowing the other's fate. Tonight they were content
to simply be near each other, and had come up with a
plan.

Admiral Buckley left Jake there and would pick
both Camille and him up on his return trip from New
Orleans. They would go back to Washington by boat
and remain there until Jake's orders came through.

It all seemed so simple. Their only concern was
about Avery—neither knew where he was. Neither had
heard from him since Camille's departure in Montgomery.

"I really think we should have gone on to New Orleans and gotten married there," said Jake as they
talked quietly.

"I'm sorry, Jake. I guess it's my fault. Things just
happened so quickly this morning, I couldn't think
straight. I guess I should've thrown a few things in a
case and forgotten about the rest. When you suggested
that we wait until Vernon returned, it just sounded so
much simpler."

"I understand. I guess I'm just a little anxious and
a lot eager." He kissed her on the tip of the nose.
"Vernon will be back in about six days if the weather
holds. I guess things will go smoother for you like
this. I'm just afraid Avery's men know I'm here, and
I've put you in danger."

Camille couldn't answer. What could she say? Both of them knew it was true. If Avery returned to the coast after Camille slipped away from the train, he would know of Jake's presence soon.

"Don't worry. Things will work out. I'll even get the local officials to guard the house if you want." Jake said it jokingly, but Camille had been thinking seriously along the same lines. Mr. Darcey had sent word that Avery's men were in the area and could cause trouble, but nothing had been done.

"I think that's a good idea. Why can't we involve them?"

Jake laughed. "Because I'm that Yankee officer they'd probably love to see murdered, remember? I'm not one of their lovable Johnny Rebs."

His sarcasm saddened Camille. She'd never heard him speak that way of the locals. She raised her eyes to see him, but didn't say a word.

"You know it's true," he said, "don't you? I have a feeling you know much too well that it's true, or you'd be with your own family and not here."

Camille looked at the floor. How could she tell him that she had lost everything because of him—even her family? He'd never believe her if she said she didn't care.

She placed her hand on Jake's face. "You've given up a lot as well. You haven't mentioned going back to Rhode Island since we've planned our future. Your family doesn't want me there, do they?"

He smiled and lifted her chin with his finger. "They'll come around. They're more upset that I'm not keeping the partnership in the bank within the family. It's a business deal to them, nothing more."

"But now you won't be with your father in the bank."

"It's not that important to me. In fact, I've never been excited about the ideas of spending my time in an office. Maybe one day, but not now. Later, when things settle down with the country and they get used to the idea of me choosing my own wife, we'll go see if Rhode Island fits us, not just me, but us. This will be your marriage and life as well."

What mattered to her right then was being with him, though her joy would only be complete if she had the blessing of her sisters and friends.

Jake pulled her to him and kissed her tenderly. "I love you, Camille. I'll make it up to you that you have to leave the home that you love, I promise."

"There's nothing to make up. I have what I want."

Chapter Fourteen

Shortly after sunrise, the smell of ham frying on the stove drifted up into her bedroom, making her stomach growl. Worrying about Jake had made her lose her appetite, but this morning she was ravenous.

She opened the curtains to a cloudy overcast sky. "This is my wedding day. How could it be cloudy?" Wrinkling her nose, she closed the curtain and refused to be anything but ecstatic.

Jake was here with her. That was all that mattered.

Gingerly she danced down the stairs and into the kitchen.

"Good morning, Alice. Breakfast smells great!"

"This is your wedding day. Everything is goin' to be good for you, honey." Alice skillfully flipped the homemade biscuits from the hot pan onto a plate. "Now, you eat up."

"Oh, I plan to. I'm starving, but I'll wait for Major Warren."

"He's waitin' for you out on the porch."

Camille's heart beat faster. "Set up our plates in the dining room. We'll be there shortly."

Jake sat on the edge of a chair with his legs spread apart, one arm resting across his leg and the other one propped on the arm of the chair. He stared out across the lawn and out into the water. Camille could tell he was worried.

"Good morning," she said as she closed the hall door behind her.

Jake's expression softened. He stood up and opened his arms to her. "Good morning." He pulled her close to him, then kissed her on the lips. "I was hoping you'd get up soon so we could eat together."

"Breakfast smells wonderful. I think Alice is trying to impress you." Camille raised her face to him to receive another quick morning kiss, then together they walked into the house.

Alice scurried back and forth from the kitchen setting plates piled high with savory breakfast foods.

"Oh, Alice, all of this looks magnificent," Camille commented on one of Alice's runs through the door. "How did you come by all this food?"

"You don't worry your head about where the food

comes from. You just enjoy. I hope you two are hungry because the Mrs. and Mr. Darcey already ate."

"Oh, my, that's a lot of food for just two people."

"Well, I don't know about you," Jake said as he pulled out a chair for Camille, "but I'm starved."

Before seating himself, he took out a revolver from his waistband and placed it on the hutch behind the table. Camille didn't say a word about the gun, but her insides tightened at the sight of it.

Jake sat next to her, placed his hand over hers, and said a quiet thank-you for food and for the two of them being together. With a quick "Amen," he squeezed her hand, then reached for a tray of ham. They served themselves in silence.

Camille took the food as Jake passed it to her, but the presence of the gun had changed her delightful morning to one of foreboding and apprehension. She tried to smile for him, but it was hard.

Jake winked at her while placing the bowl of grits in her hand. "Don't look so scared, Camille. It'll all work out. We have to give it time."

"I didn't know it showed."

"Show? It's written all over your face."

"I'm sorry. I don't mean to be depressing, but I guess I'm more frightened about all this than I thought."

Jake stopped serving himself. "Are you scared to marry me?"

"Oh, no," Camille jumped in. "Never. I've been ready to marry you for longer than I would admit it to myself. I love you. It's the other business that has my insides knotting."

"Avery?"

She nodded.

"You have a right to be scared about that. That's the reason for the gun, but I swear, Camille, if there's anything I can do to protect you, I will. We'll get through this thing together."

He leaned over and held her.

"Why can't it just be the two of us?"

He didn't answer, but held her close until she was ready to continue breakfast.

They ate quietly and tried to discuss their course of action sensibly. It seemed so simple as long as Avery stayed out of the picture. After they finished their meal, Jake helped her with her chair. When she turned, Jake had a big smile on his face.

"What are you smiling about?"

"You," he said. "You've eaten as much as I have. I didn't know a little body like yours could hold so much food!"

"Jake Warren, that's not a nice thing to say about your future wife."

He laughed. "Come on. Let's help Alice get these things cleaned up. If we stay busy, we'll feel better."

Camille threw her arms around him. "God, I'm glad you're here with me. I've prayed so hard."

He kissed her on the forehead. "I'm here. Let's hope all of your prayers are answered."

Together they began to pick up dishes when the kitchen door flew open. A man holding his hand over Alice's mouth pushed her through the door, a gun pointed to her side. Avery stepped in next with a rifle pointing right at Jake and Camille.

A strange guttural sound escaped from Camille, but she managed not to scream. She felt Jake stiffen.

"Don't move, Major Warren, or your little lady there will have a hole in that pretty body of hers."

Avery's breaths came in gulps, and sweat ran down his face. His whole body trembled.

Camille swallowed hard. Avery was nervous. The man's condition could work either way for Jake. It could slow his reflexes or it could make him irrational and dangerous.

"What do you want, Avery?" Jake asked sounding cool and unmoved.

"Oh, I think you know what I want. I've come for what's mine."

"There's nothing here that's yours, so take your friend and go before someone gets hurt."

Avery laughed. "You're wrong, Warren. You're mine. You owe me a lot, and I'm going to take it out of you a little at a time. Each hole in you will repay me for this scar on my face, my men you killed, and those months I sat in your rat hole of a dungeon." He grunted. "Oh, you owe me a lot. Then your little lady here owes me for sneaking out on me."

"You leave her out of this. We'll settle things if you think a duel's in order, but you leave her out."

Avery laughed again. "A duel? I didn't say nothing about no gentleman's duel. You're not going to have a chance to defend yourself, Warren."

With those words Avery's gun fired, but Camille didn't hear the explosion. Her hand flew to her mouth. As if in slow motion, the scene replayed itself again and again in a matter of seconds—the red discharge from the gun barrel, Jake being lifted off his feet and into the hutch. Avery's sadistic smile.

Her body froze in a state of disbelief and shock. Then without thinking, she grabbed the gun on the hutch, aimed, and fired.

Avery's smile turned into an expression of shock. With a thud, he fell to the floor.

Avery's partner, standing in stunned amazement, threw Alice aside. When Camille pointed the weapon at him, he dropped his own gun. "Don't shoot."

The kitchen door flew open again and the Darceys bounded through with Mr. Darcey carrying a gun.

"It's okay," Camille shouted to them and, seeing his gun, she dropped hers on the table and ran to Jake.

He lay with his head against the table. Blood oozed down onto the floor from his head. She lifted him to her body. "Oh God, don't let him be . . ." But she couldn't say the last word. Her body crumpled around him, cradling his head against her chest, but when she felt his warm breath, she burst into tears.

Mrs. Darcey and Alice knelt by her. "Oh, Camille," and "Oh, Jake" was all Camille made out.

"He's alive," Camille said through her tears. "Help me with him."

"Wait until Mr. Darcey can help so we don't hurt him," Mrs. Darcey said patting Jake's face.

Camille examined his head where blood was seeping. The wound wasn't bad.

"His leg's bleeding," Alice almost screamed in a high-pitched voice.

Camille placed Jake's head down gently on the floor, then grabbed his leg. "Quick, get a cloth. We need to get the bleeding under control." She started pressure on the wound, then ripped open the trouser fabric when Alice brought in a cloth.

"He must've hit his head when he fell," suggested Mrs. Darcey.

Camille nodded. She cleaned around the wound and expertly applied pressure. Knowing the extent of the wound relieved her mind, and she was able to work unemotionally.

Jake was going to live.

He had come for her, knowing that Avery would probably be here. Had she listened to him and boarded Captain Buckley's ship that day, this could've been avoided. It tore at her heart to know his life had been in danger.

She had never shot anyone in her life, but she was glad that she had shot Avery. He was scum, but as soon as the realization of what she'd done registered in her brain, a shudder ran through her body. She turned to see Mr. Darcey kneel down by Avery's massive body.

"Unfortunately, the rascal will live," he mumbled as he stuck a cloth against his side.

Glad that she hadn't killed a man, Camille turned away and ministered to Jake.

After Mrs. Darcey consoled Alice and helped Mr. Darcey, she knelt down by Camille and placed her arm around Camille's shoulder. "It looks like he's going to be all right. You're both very lucky."

"Yes, ma'am, I know we are. Jake could have been killed."

"You both could have been killed, but now he's going to be better soon. Mr. Darcey will help us move him shortly."

"Thank you," Camille said and smiled up at the lady who pampered her. She was lucky to have Mr. and Mrs. Darcey, and one day she hoped to thank them properly.

Jake lay unmoving while Camille continued the pressure on his thigh.

Mrs. Darcey spoke quietly to her husband. Camille was unable to make out what they were saying, but she was sure something was wrong. Her heart pounded in her chest.

Finally Mr. Darcey knelt by Camille. "Avery will live. He and his friend are tied up with Alice holding a gun on them. I've sent Joseph across the bay for the sheriff."

"Do you think there'll be trouble, you know, having Jake here and all?" she asked.

"No, darling, that man broke into my home. I, you, or Jake had a right to shoot him. No trouble will be had." He positioned his arm around Jake's shoulder and tried to lift him. "Right now, we need to get him off the floor. When he wakes up, I'm not sure what's going to hurt worse, his head or his leg."

It took three of them to carry Jake over to the couch in the parlor. With Mr. Darcey hardly able to get around alone, trying to get Jake up the stairs into a bed was out of the question.

Camille finished dressing the flesh wound on his leg and putting a bandage on his head. Jake moaned and tried to move. She moved closer to him as he opened his eyes.

"Hello," Camille whispered. "How do you feel?"

"What happened?" he mumbled, but immediately squeezed his eyes shut. Before Camille could answer, his eyes flew open. "Avery! Where's Avery?"

Jake tried to get up, but his hands went to each side of his head. Camille leaned over him and gently placed him back onto the couch.

"Everything's fine, Jake. Go back to sleep. Everyone's safe."

Jake lay unmoving for several minutes, then he opened his eyes again. This time without moving, he asked again where Avery was.

"Avery's tied up. The sheriff's on his way."

"What happened?" he asked in a whisper.

Camille swallowed hard. "I shot him."

He reached for her hand. "How did that happen?"

"You were knocked out."

He grimaced. "How did I manage to get myself knocked out?"

"Well, you didn't exactly do it, Jake. Avery was playing a cruel game with you. He was going to shoot you in a lot of places and let you die slowly, but when he shot you in the leg, you fell and hit the hutch."

Jake managed to look down at his leg and frowned.

"You're probably lucky that you were knocked out. There's no telling what would've happened. You probably would've tried to take him on with an injured leg. You might have been killed."

She stopped and looked him in the eyes.

"So in the meantime, while I'm lying on the ground helpless, you just happened to shoot him," he said with a bit of sarcasm.

"There wasn't anything else to do." There was no way to hide the hurt in her voice.

He took her hand and squeezed it. "I'm sorry. I'm not being fair to you. I'm aggravated with myself. I can't believe I came all the way over here to protect you, and you wound up protecting me." He tried to shake his head but closed his eyes tightly and moaned.

"Would you be still?" she said and put a hand on his face. "You officers aren't very good patients."

He held her hand against his cheek until he was able to talk again. "I'm so sorry I wasn't there for you."

"What's the difference who shot him? It's over and now he'll be put in prison. We can live in peace."

"You're right. I'm sorry." His voice was getting weaker. "You said the sheriff was on his way?"

"Yes. Joseph went after him."

"Will you help me up so I can talk to him."

This time Camille pushed against his chest. "Lie down, Jake Warren. You're going to stay right here. If the sheriff wants to talk with you, he can come in here."

She leaned over him and kissed him on the lips. He struggled to open his eyes.

"Please stay put. It took a while to get the bleeding under control. I'd hate for you to reopen the wound."

Jake didn't argue. Camille dipped a cloth in a bowl of water and placed it on his forehead.

"There's not much I can do for the pain. If you can suggest something that might help, I'll do it. If not, the best thing for you to do is to sleep."

Jake didn't answer. He lay perfectly still, and after a few minutes Camille realized he was asleep.

The business with the sheriff didn't take long. With

the Darceys demanding action, the sheriff agreed to do everything in his power to get Avery and his man into a federal prison.

After making sure his two prisoners were secure in the wagon, the sheriff walked over to Camille again. He lit a cigar and leaned up against the railing of the porch. "After you and your friend get married, are you staying around here?"

"No, I don't think so. I feel sure we'll go back to Washington."

"Good. We have enough Yankees around here, and I'm sure your neighbors would appreciate you following him up North if that's what you have in your head to do."

His change of tone shocked Camille. "Sir, I don't appreciate . . ."

But the squatty sheriff cut her off. "No, ma'am, you don't seem to understand. *We* don't appreciate what you're doing. Your brother died in that man's prison camp, and here you are ignoring that and marrying that Yankee officer anyway."

Camille grabbed the railing for support at the mention of her brother's death. "Sir, my sisters and I still mourn my brother's death. My mother gave up living. His death has not been taken lightly, but I don't blame Major Warren."

Mr. Darcey stepped up behind the sheriff. "I think your job is finished here. You and your men need to get off this property."

"Yes, sir, Mr. Darcey, I'm going. I don't want to cause you and your wife any trouble. That's why I'm telling this lady to get her man and leave the area. There'll be trouble if she stays and you know it."

"We don't need to be told what we know or don't know, sir. Now, I appreciate that you came to get Avery and his partner, but I will now bid you good-bye. Your job is done."

The sheriff tipped his hat to Mrs. Darcey and addressed Camille again. "You do what I say. You don't want to cause these good people any trouble. There's a group of locals that seem to do what they want, and what they want is to get rid of all these here carpetbaggers. If you want to keep your man alive, you'd better get him away from here."

Once more the sheriff tipped his hat to the ladies then left.

Mr. Darcey put his arm around Camille. "Now, honey, don't you let that man scare you. You and Jake are welcome here as long as you want."

"I know that. I do thank you, but what he says is true. No, after we get married . . ." She stopped abruptly and looked at Jake. "Oh, my, we were going to get married today."

"That's not a problem," Mrs. Darcey said. "I'll send Joseph or Leon to tell the priest not to come today. There'll be time before the ship comes back."

She nodded. "I don't want to cause you trouble like the sheriff said. Both of you have been so kind to

Jake and me. We'll move on as soon as Admiral Buckley returns for us."

Mr. Darcey looked up. "Let's get you inside. It looks like we're in for a nice rainstorm, but you remember that you and the major are welcome here anytime."

A sense of dread and loneliness swept over her as she approached the house. This wonderful land would never be hers again. Even though the Darceys still welcomed her into their home, no one else did. She was being thrown out as if she were as rotten as Avery and his men were, and her only crime was loving someone who called the North home.

Five years ago it would have been acceptable to love him. Today it was not. The war might have ended, but the hatred and distrust still existed.

After checking on Jake, she walked to the window and pulled aside the heavy drapes. Ominous black clouds swept across the sky as they had on the day that her family had been caught in the small boat. She shivered and welcomed the calm of the big house.

Reminiscent of the nights she sat by Jake in the fort, Camille stayed by Jake's side well into the night, sometimes accompanied by Mr. or Mrs. Darcey, sometimes alone.

She left his side at one point and helped Mr. Darcey and Joseph prepare for the bad weather. They closed shutters, stored items in the yard, and took care of the boat and horses. Low clouds covered the moon, making the yard dark and threatening, and before they finished, the rain came down in sheets.

"Come on inside, Camille. The rest can stay. Maybe this will blow over," he yelled over the rain and wind, but neither Mr. Darcey nor Camille believed it.

Her stomach churned. The coast hadn't had a bad storm in a number of years. She prayed this wasn't one. With so much happening, she didn't think she could endure much more.

The big grandfather clock in the hallway struck 3 o'clock as Camille curled up in the settee in the parlor, but the howling of the wind and brushing of the oak limbs against the house kept her wide-awake.

Several times during the evening, she felt as if the house itself vibrated. One small candle burned on the table, making shadows dance across the ceiling and sending chills through her body. How she wanted to climb up next to Jake and cuddle, but she knew that sleep was the best thing for him.

The Darceys checked on her periodically and offered to sit with Jake again, but she refused to leave him.

Thunder crashed and a flash of lightning lit the room. Camille jumped.

"Are you all right?" Jake asked, sounding groggy.

Camille kneeled next to the couch. "I'm fine. You rest."

"Sounds like we're having some bad weather," he said with his eyes barely open.

"That's an understatement if I ever heard one. I really think we're getting into a full-fledged storm."

Another crash of thunder made Camille wrap her arms around herself tightly.

"Come closer."

When Jake reached for her, she leaned into him and buried her face in the crook of his neck.

"I like having you hold me. It makes me feel safe."

"And I like holding you." He inhaled deeply. "I hate lying here. Did anyone help Mr. Darcey get things secured?"

"Joseph and I did, but the weather didn't get bad until after the sun set." She rubbed her hand over his face. "Please don't worry about anything. You couldn't have gotten up even if you'd been awake."

He took her hand and moved it to his lips. "You do realize that this was supposed to be your wedding night?" he said softly.

"*Our* wedding night. How could I forget?" She sighed. "We've waited this long. I guess a few more days won't hurt us as long as we're together. That's all that matters to me right now. Having you by my side is enough for me right now."

She lifted her face and kissed him lightly on the lips, but as she tried to move away, he placed his hand on the back of her head and held her as he kissed her passionately.

Her body ached for Jake to continue, to have him

as close to her as he could get. Good sense took over and she pulled away.

Another crash of thunder sent Camille back into his arms. It felt good to have someone console her for a change, and as he held her, she didn't fight the sleep that tugged at her eyelids.

Chapter Fifteen

Camille sensed it was near morning even though no light shone through the shutters.

"Good morning, sleepy head." Jake's deep voice drew her out of the last bit of sleep.

"I don't want to move. You feel too good," she mumbled.

"I know. I haven't felt this good waking up in a long time, even with two new holes in my body."

Camille's eyes flew open when she remembered why she was sitting on the floor with her head in Jake's arms. "Oh, tell me I didn't hurt you."

"You didn't hurt me. You've been a real still sleeper." He smiled and kissed her on the forehead.

"Sounds like the Darceys are up and moving. Let's

go see what they're doing. They might need some help." Jake tried to lift himself.

"You can't get up."

"Let's try. If I think I'll make things worse, I'll get back on the couch. I promise. Now give me a hand."

Clinging to her, he managed to stand. Keeping one hand on Camille's shoulder and using the other to support himself on the furniture, he was able to take a few steps.

"Your head is as hard as that gun barrel, Major Warren."

Jake grunted. "I wish it was. Maybe it wouldn't hurt so dang bad."

Mr. and Mrs. Darcey met them at the door.

"Lord, have mercy!" exclaimed Mrs. Darcey. "Have you two lost your minds?"

"You know men, Mrs. Darcey. They refuse to be pampered, especially this one."

Mr. Darcey reached out and helped Jake to a chair at the door of the parlor. "He'll be fine, Mama. The man can't rest when there's a storm about to tear into this house."

Mr. Darcey poured two glasses of sherry from the sidebar. "This ought to help your leg and might even help you forget your headache. For me, well, it'll just help." He laughed, then took a big swallow.

Another loud crash of thunder exploded nearby.

Camille seated herself next to Jake and accepted a taste of sherry from his glass.

"Is there anything we can do?" Jake asked.

"No, not now. I'm sure there'll be lots to do when this thing passes. You two relax a little. The missus and me are going out to the kitchen to round up some food."

They left them alone.

"What are you thinking about?" Jake asked as he tried to find a comfortable position for his leg.

"I'm worried about my sisters and the shop. When I was small, a storm knocked the house next to ours off its foundation and the water rose so high, it got into our house. I'm scared that Paul won't know what to do. He's not from the coast."

"I'm sure he'll do fine. Anyway, your house looks pretty sturdy."

"Yes, but the shop is right on the water. If it's damaged, they won't have any income."

Jake pulled her next to him. "We'll go over in the morning and check on them, but right now there's nothing you can do about it. Try to relax."

"I will, but only because you're here."

He raised her face to his and kissed her. "I love you so much."

She kissed him back, then snuggled up again and soon let herself drift into sleep.

The fury of the wind could still be heard even as

the day began to break, but then suddenly it became silent and still outside.

"We're in the eye," Camille whispered.

"I know. I might be from Rhode Island, but once in a while we do get storms that reach us up there." He said it with a grin on his face.

She left to get coffee. When she returned, she sat next to him, waiting for the back side of the storm to hit.

"What's on your mind, Camille? You look like you're about to burst."

"Did you mean what you said about taking me across the bay to see Dorothy and Katherine?"

"Of course I meant it, but we have to wait until this side of the storm passes. Just as soon as I think it's safe, I'll ask Joseph to get the boat ready. You'll see. They'll all be fine."

Camille settled her head against him and wondered just how fine they'd be seeing Jake with her. In fact, she wondered if they even knew she had returned to the area.

By midmorning the worst of the winds had passed, and as soon as the rains stopped, the sun peeked around the wall of clouds that moved inland. It always amazed Camille how quickly the storms came and how quickly they left.

Camille and Jake stood on the pier waiting for Mr. Darcey and Joseph to put the boat in the water for them.

"Are you sure you don't need me to come with you?" Mr. Darcey asked as Joseph tied the boat up to the pier.

"No, sir," Jake answered. "I think I can handle this."

Jake had done so much for her already, Camille prayed she hadn't asked too much of him. Logs and parts of trees washed past them. "Maybe we shouldn't go," she said.

Jake held out his hand to her. "If you want to check on your family, we have to go. We'll be able to keep the boat afloat, I promise."

He winked at her and her heart overflowed with love for him.

"If you two are going, you'd best leave now."

"Okay, Mr. Darcey, I can see you're trying to get rid of us." She kissed him on the cheek, then got into the boat.

She and Joseph had to help Jake. His jaw muscles tightened and twitched as he stepped in and sat.

"Jake, maybe we shouldn't . . ."

"We're going. Now hand me an oar. It's my leg and head that hurt, not my arms. I promise I can row."

He pushed them away from the pier and immediately the current pulled the boat into its stream. There wouldn't be much effort to move the boat, but keeping it on course would be another matter.

Jake struggled with the oars as the current swept the boat through the water. Camille tried to help, but knew she was in the way. Her heart poured out to him for doing this, especially knowing that he would not be welcomed when they got to the other side. She was sure he knew it as well. His pain from the boat ride and the rejection that awaited him made her hate being pulled by this need to see to her family.

As she got closer to her home, she reached over and grabbed Jake's hand. The shoreline of the bay across from the opening of the two landmasses had taken the full force of the winds and high tide, but her shop and home still stood.

Jake grabbed her hand as they got closer and were able to see that a huge pecan tree lay across the top of the house.

"Oh, please don't let them have been in there during the storm," she prayed out loud.

"There's someone walking around the front of the house," Jake said as he fought to keep the boat on course.

"It looks like Paul. Oh, please let my sisters be okay."

Jake guided the boat to the pier by the shop. The small pier next to it that had jutted out from her lawn for as long as she could remember was completely gone. Only the pilings remained.

Camille tried to run to the house through the wet seaweed that had been washed ashore, but stopped when she realized that Jake couldn't move very fast.

"Go on. I'll catch up with you."

She turned and smiled at him, and without saying anything she ran to the house.

Paul stood alongside the building with another man examining the damage.

"Paul! Paul!" she shouted as she ran up to the two.

Paul turned around and opened his arms to her. Grateful for his display of emotion, she accepted this embrace. "Where're Dorothy and Katherine? Tell me they're okay."

"They're just fine, but Dorothy was so shook up that I took them up to the Rices' as soon as the weather broke."

Camille's hands flew to her mouth. "You mean you stayed here last night?"

Paul nodded with a look of embarrassment. "I didn't know, Camille. We've never had to leave up where we live. I just didn't know it was going to be this bad. By the time I decided that I should leave, it was too dangerous. I'm thankful no one was hurt." He looked up and saw Jake limping around the corner of the house. He stiffened. "Did you have to bring him?"

"Look, Paul, he was concerned about you and my sisters as much as I was, so please be cordial to him. Please," she begged.

"I don't have to be cordial to any Yankee, Camille. He has no right here."

"He has as much right as I do. He's going to be my husband."

Even that didn't affect him, though, for when Jake walked up behind them, Paul turned and walked away.

"Well, I can see he's overjoyed to see me. He wasn't rude to you, was he?"

"Oh, no, but you're right, he isn't real happy that you're here."

"Happy or not, I'm here and I might as well give them a hand." He walked over to Paul and another man and stood back as they threw a rope around the end of the tree that lay across the roof.

Camille followed him and touched his arm. "Would you come with me to see about the shop while they're securing the tree? I couldn't tell if there was any damage done to it or not."

Together they walked through the slushy lawn, carefully avoiding the driftwood and other debris that had been washed ashore. Camille had to shove to get the shop door open and gasped as soon as she stepped in. No outward signs of damage could be seen, but as soon as the swollen door was pushed open, it was obvious that the water of the bay had been inside the shop.

Dorothy and Paul had not picked up any of the supplies on the floor because nets, spools of twine, needles, stools, and anything else that had been near or on the floor had been washed into one corner of the building, now covered with seaweed and mud. A huge cockroach crawled around the edge of the pile.

Jake put his arm around her. "I'm so sorry."

Camille couldn't answer, but the stunned look on her face told Jake how she felt. Her gaze followed the floor line where the force of the rising water had gushed through the minute cracks in the wooden floor, causing the boards to warp and twist.

"We'll get it back to normal. We won't leave your building like this." Jake tried to console her.

Camille took a deep breath, threw her shoulders back, and shook her head. "I've never seen such a mess."

Jake laughed.

"Why are you laughing?"

"I'm laughing at you. It's your reaction to things. Just when I think I have you figured out and think I can predict your next move, you fool me."

"Well, would you rather that I cry?"

"Lord, no, but that's what I was expecting." He reached over and gave her a quick hug. "I'm glad I'm here with you."

Camille smiled. "Thank you, Jake. I need you here because had I not gotten mad, I really would've cried. That's what I feel like doing."

She turned her attention from the shop. "Do you think we can help them before we leave?"

"I wouldn't have it any other way." He looked around. "I'm not sure where to start, but we'll do what we can to help them get all this back in order."

For the next three days, Jake and Camille and even Joseph, Leon, and Mr. Darcey at times, helped in the shop and at the house. Paul completely ignored Jake for the first two days. It was all Camille could do to keep from yelling at Paul to make him see how childish he was being.

Each time, Jake told her to forget it.

In the evening Joseph rowed them across the bay as they sat exhausted on the wooden benches. Camille knew that Jake's injuries were still painful, but he kept his pain to himself until they got in the boat alone. It was as if he could finally close his eyes and groan or rub his leg and curse the pain, and it would be okay.

Camille understood. "I wish there was something I could do for your leg, but you know you're only hurting yourself by doing all this."

"This is something I want to do."

It was the same every night, but every morning he would hobble down the pier and go across the bay again. Many times during the day she watched him grab a tree or a railing for support as a weak spell passed through him or pain shot up his leg.

On the third day of their cleaning, Camille walked out to the well to get some fresh water. Paul was dipping water and pouring it over his head.

"Hot morning, already, isn't it?" she said to Paul to make pleasant conversation. What she wanted to do was to stick his head in the well until he saw Jake for what he really was.

"The cleaning's hard enough, but this heat is really getting to me."

"Paul, you know Jake is still healing from what Avery did to us. He was here for my protection so I wish you'd be a little kinder to him. The man's still in a lot of pain."

"Look, Camille, I appreciate all he's doing, but no one invited him here. He can go back to New York or wherever it is that he's from and no one will care. Let him recuperate elsewhere."

"That's not the point. He's here because of me. You're my family. He's never done anything to you. I can't understand why you feel this way about him, especially when he saved all of our land for us."

"You can't understand, huh? Well, I'll tell you why." He threw the last of the water from the dipper on the ground. When he looked back at her his eyes were red with anger. "It was Yankees like him who made me crawl through mud like an animal and nearly starve to death during the war. My family suffered. Your family suffered. Charles died under him, and yet you ask why I don't like the bluecoat."

"I feel sorry for you, Paul." Her temper teetered on the brink of explosion. "I really do feel sorry for you. The war's over. Let this hate die. Let's bury it along with everything else we've buried."

Paul glared at her, then turned and left without another word. Camille picked up the empty bucket and pumped. As the water splashed into the bucket, an overwhelming helpless feeling settled over her.

This was her life, her family, and her friends, but she would have to leave it all forever because people like Paul would keep the hate alive forever.

If her mind hadn't been made up before, it certainly was now. She would leave with Jake as soon as Vernon returned with his ship, and she doubted she'd ever come back. Jake would be her life now, and no matter how much she loved this area, she would have to replace it with Jake's life.

His love was worth more than this, and making him suffer this humiliation was not fair.

When her bucket was full, she moved and pumped more water and let it run over her arms. The cool well water loosened the gray muck that caked on everything and ran down her arms.

"I think I could use some of that water. I have mud from one end of me to the other."

Camille looked up and saw Jake. "I didn't hear you walk up."

"I know. You were in awfully deep thoughts there. You and Paul must have had quite a talk."

Camille tried to hide her feelings.

"Let it drop, Camille. You're only hurting yourself. Paul and these others don't want to listen to you right now." He touched her hands with his wet one as the water ran over them. "These men are still hurting on the inside, but they aren't hurting me."

"But they're hurting me, because whether you admit it or not, it's got to bother you. Why won't they listen to me? Why won't they give you a chance?"

Jake placed a damp arm around her and pulled her to him. "Oh, my little idealist. I just wish more people were like you. This world would be a much better place."

"I want to get married."

"Well, I hope so," he said with a big grin.

"No, I want to get married tomorrow. We were supposed to get married three days ago before all this mess happened. Let's forget all this and do it tomorrow."

He smiled down at her. "Whatever you want, but just make sure you won't feel guilty later on, you know, about leaving all this work."

She shook her head. "No, I won't feel guilty about leaving it. What I'll probably feel guilty about is having put you through all this for my stubborn family."

"Don't worry about my feelings. I've put them aside a long time ago—except for you, of course."

"I do have one more favor to ask. We have a couple of hours before Joseph comes after us. Would you walk down the road to the cemetery with me? I want to tell Charles, Mama, and Papa good-bye."

Jake stayed close by Camille as she laid wild flowers on the graves.

He had told her not to worry, but Jake worried enough for both of them. He worried that Camille would miss her family when they left. He worried that Paul would do something really stupid and make him lose his temper. So far Jake had refused to react to Paul's rebuffs outwardly because of Camille, digging deep within himself to find the strength to ignore his jabs.

He'd worked with misplaced Southerners in Washington. He'd gotten used to the resentment, but coming from Paul made it difficult to ignore. Paul's behavior hurt Camille. Not wanting to cause problems before he left, he'd stood silent as he watched Camille's eyes fill with tears. His insides boiled.

For the next several hours they worked side by side. Dorothy and Katherine had returned to the house during the day. Camille and he found them cleaning the inside rooms that were not under the damaged roof. She told them she and Jake would not return.

Katherine threw her arms around Camille. "Oh, I can't bear to see you go."

"I'll be fine, Katherine, and so will you. It's better this way."

"I can't blame you." Dorothy looked Jake straight in the eye. "I didn't want you here either, Mr. Warren, but I've come to realize that you're a good man." She looked at the floor. "I'm sorry about the way my husband is acting. He is my husband, though. I can't go against him."

"I understand," Jake answered, but left the rest go. What he understood was that Paul's hatred was splitting up sisters who loved each other.

Jake returned to the yard, leaving the sisters to say their good-byes.

The tree had been taken down from the house and

the men had worked on roof repairs all day. Jake stayed on the ground because of his leg. Even with the other neighbors gone, Paul remained on the roof. When Joseph was spotted coming across the channel, Jake and Camille gathered their things.

Dorothy and Katherine walked them to the water's edge. Dorothy looked up at her husband working alone.

"I'm sure he'll stay up there 'til you leave just so he won't have to say anything to you."

"Don't worry about it," Jake answered a little too quickly. By now his leg ached and the only thing he wanted to do was to sit in the boat.

Dorothy and Katherine took turns hugging Camille, but before the boat got to the pier, a loud crash and scream erupted. The girls ran toward the house. Jake hobbled as fast as he could. When he got to the house, he saw Paul hanging on with only the top portion of his body showing out of the roof.

With Camille's help, Jake moved the ladder nearer to him. "Hold on, Paul," Jake yelled but wondered if his own leg would support him on a weakened roof.

"I can't hold much longer. The beams are gone under me. There's nothing to put my foot on," Paul yelled down.

"Try not to move," Jake yelled back and dragged his injured leg up one rung of the ladder onto the next until he reached the roofline. Sweat poured off his face.

Paul clung to the edge of the damaged section with whitened fingers, his face pale.

Jake struggled to get off the ladder, then slid along the incline of the roofline. "Are you hurt?"

Paul managed to shake his head.

Jake could tell Paul couldn't hold on much longer. He prayed for strength to pull his future brother-in-law out. "Take my hand."

Paul strained to reach Jake's hand. "I can't."

Jake took several deep breaths to ward off the pain that shot through his leg with each move. He scooted closer to Paul. When Paul grabbed his hand, Jake put his head down in the crook of his arm to get control of his own body.

When he raised his head, Jake's gaze met Paul's. For a long second, Jake didn't move. The sweat running down his arm saturated his hand. He felt Paul slipping.

Both men knew Jake could let Paul fall to his death by simply not moving, but in another instant, Jake pulled his own body closer to Paul's and reached for him with his other hand.

Paul struggled, pulling up out of the hole until he lay across the roof next to Jake. Jake's body still quivered from the pain in his leg, but he never let go of Paul's hand.

"The ladder's right under us," Jake managed to say. "You'll have to get there on your own."

Paul nodded with an embarrassed thank-you in his eyes.

After Paul was safely down, Jake shimmied down the roofline until he reached the ladder. With Camille holding it steady, he got down one rung at a time until he fell into Camille's arms and they toppled to the ground together.

Camille buried her face in his chest. "Oh, God, you could've fallen." She sobbed, and Jake let her. He didn't have the strength or the inclination to hide the way he felt. He had put on a facade for too long.

"Where's Paul?" he asked.

"He and Dorothy went inside," she said though her sniffles.

"Is he all right?"

"Yes, but he didn't wait around to make sure you were."

Jake held her close to him. From now on, he would be her family. These people didn't deserve her.

Chapter Sixteen

"**Y**ou happy?"

"You know I am. I've never been so content." Camille leaned her head against the fine hair on Jake's chest and took a deep breath. After yesterday's humiliating happenings with her brother-in-law, this day had been wonderful.

Jake and Camille had risen early, then drove the Darcey carriage down the Spanish Trail to Mobile where they were married by a chubby little pastor on the outskirts of town. It had been a quick, simple ceremony with the gardener and his wife going into the church to stand for them.

Nothing else was needed. Jake carried with him a plain gold band and as he placed it on Camille's finger, she had to force back the tears of joy. After all

259

the disasters they'd been through to get here, she was glad the moment wasn't crowded with too much ceremony. Jake was all she wanted.

Afterward, they found a room in one of the old mansions along Springhill Avenue, and then walked hand in hand along the lovely flower-lined streets of Mobile. Most of the old mansions had remained intact throughout the war, and now, even though most of the original owners had been forced away by taxes, the buildings showed signs of restoration.

Camille oohed and aahed at the great columns and ornate handiwork that decorated most of the buildings.

Jake took her into a dress shop, and when they reentered the sunny street, he carried three boxes, each containing a new ready-made item he insisted she buy. Since the war had ended, Camille had acquired pieces of fabric from peddlers and had made herself several outfits, but she had never owned a new ready-made dress or cape.

Letting someone else take care of her was a new experience for Camille. She barely remembered a time when the burden of her family hadn't been on her shoulders, and having Jake pamper her as he was doing soothed her.

The carriage ride back to the Darceys', final packing, and the return of Buckley's ship all happened so quickly that Camille didn't have time to think much about leaving her home.

Buckley arrived in one of his larger sloops. They

wasted no time in boarding. As the sloop turned into the wind and headed south into the Sound, Camille felt as though she was losing the only world she'd ever known.

Jake grabbed her hand.

No word could ease the moment, but with Jake next to her, Camille sat straight and tall and let the beach line and her old life fade. The strained moment passed.

"I love you, Camille. I'd do anything to keep you from hurting. If you need to go back, I'll get Vernon to turn the boat around. I came through a war for you. I can do anything right now just to know that you love me."

Camille's chest tightened with the love that overwhelmed her. "No. I have everything I need right here."

He nodded. "Thank you. I do too."

They sat holding hands in silence as the sloop slid across the water to the ship where the activity of transferring trunks and bags momentarily took away Camille's remorse. Vernon escorted them into his quarters, and as the ship headed south away from her home, they shared a light meal of meat and fruit.

"I hope you don't mind, but I have a quick stop to make at Ship Island. I have a load of supplies to deliver to the fort supervisor today. Won't take long for a quick hello."

"Not at all," Jake replied. "I'd kind of like to see the old fort again. How about you, Camille?"

"I'd like that. I'd even like to walk on the beach once more. Who knows when I'll be able to ever do that again."

"Hey, we have beaches up north too, you know. I think you'll be pleasantly surprised."

Vernon pushed back his chair. "I think we can arrange for you two to have a little time on the island. I'll take my time if you two aren't in a hurry. Ole Buckeye and me go a long way back. I look forward to visiting with the old cogger when I make these runs. He usually has a pot of beans on the stove and the strongest, worst coffee you've ever tasted." He slapped the tabletop. "We'll sail with the tide."

Vernon anchored about one-fourth of a mile off the island's white beaches, and two small boats were lowered to transport them and the supplies.

As they neared the island, Camille was surprised to see that most of the prison structures had been removed or destroyed with the recent storm, leaving miles of undisturbed white sand. It was hard to believe that thousands of men suffered through the duration of their captivity here, many having died here as Charles had. She closed her eyes and said a silent prayer for her brother and for the men she never met.

None of that suffering was visible now. The white sands glistened and the water sparkled as it gently lapped against the beach.

"It's so different," Camille said as they stepped off the boat.

"Yes" was all Jake said.

They met Buckeye, and after having a cup of coffee with him in the fort's courtyard, Camille and Jake walked alone. This time it was Jake's turn to be silent. He looked in at his old room, visited the vacant dungeon, and inspected the massive structure, silently recalling events that happened in each place.

As they headed toward the steps to go to the top of the fort, Vernon called out to Jake. Camille stood at the foot of the circular stairs and watched as Vernon handed Jake a piece of paper. When he returned, he took her hand and led her to the top of the fort, climbing the steep, circular steps.

Camille had never been this high in her life. Breathtakingly, the entire outline of the island stretched out before them. The cool breeze caressed her as she surveyed the miles of beach surrounding the inland marshes and the tall pines that grew along the far end of the island.

"It's beautiful."

"Yes, it is. I used to stand up here and try to imagine what it would be like out here without the constant reminders of war. My favorite time was just before sunset." He placed his arm around her shoulders. "Sometimes I used to come up here and stand alone and take in the beauty. It was so quiet, so removed from the prisoners below. After I met you, I used to look toward the coastline and think about you."

"Oh, you didn't."

"Why would you say that?"

"I don't know. I just never thought about men having romantic thoughts."

"Camille, if I hadn't had something to think about other than this war, I would've lost my mind. Even before I knew I loved you, I thought about you."

Camille looked toward the North, to her homeland stretched out in the distance. Only a narrow strip of trees took shape along the horizon, but in her heart she could see all the scattered structures that lined the beach.

Jake held out an envelope. "Vernon asked me to give this to you. Your sister sent it to Mrs. Darcey, but Vernon forgot to give it to you earlier. I hope it's nothing upsetting."

Camille stared at the envelope, almost afraid to read what was inside. She held it to her body.

"You'll never know until you open it."

Slowly, she broke away the seal. Unfolding the page, she saw the delicate handwriting of her younger sister.

My dearest sister,

It's hard to believe that you will be leaving me soon, and that I will not be able to give you the proper farewell that you so deserve. There is so much that needs to be said, but there is not enough time or words to say it. Just let me say that I have admired you always—keeping the

*family going during the war, surviving the lone-
liness of being away from the man you love, and
starting the business alone.*

*You always were the strong one. Now, you
again are the strong one, for as I stand here, too
weak and afraid to go to you as I should, you are
starting on an adventure with the one you love
even though you have no support from your family or friends.*

*You and Jake will be happy together. In my
heart I know that your destiny together will be a
good one.*

*I apologize again for the actions of my hus-
band, as well as others in the community, but let
me say that I expect them to change one day. Paul
could never face your husband now with the
thanks he so deserves, but I heard him tell someone how the major saved him, and it seemed that
his tone had softened. He is a proud man. We are
a proud South, but in time, my dear Camille, I
know that you and Jake will be able to return to
your beloved home and be welcomed. Let us pray
that it will not be long.*

*Katherine and I will think of you often. I pray
for your happiness.*

                    Your loving sister, Dorothy

Camille stood and looked out across the water,
tears flowing down her hot face. Her insides ached,

not from sorrow, but from joy, an indescribable joy mixed with yearnings, love, and happiness.

She wanted to reach out and touch the land that lay across the water, but it lay separated from her, not just by physical miles but by years of prejudice and hatred.

One day, though, she and Jake would return. She knew that they would, and more important, she knew that they could.